12 Bodies
and a Wedding
(a Body Movers novel)

STEPHANIE BOND

CHAPTER 1

You're invited to
the wedding of

Carlotta Wren
&
Dr. Cooper Craft

SATURDAY THE TWELFTH
OF JUNE
AT THREE O'CLOCK
IN THE AFTERNOON

THE GEORGIAN TERRACE HOTEL
ATLANTA, GA

Reception to follow

"WOW, THAT was quick," Hannah Kizer said, handing the wedding invitation back to Carlotta. "Coop proposed, what a week ago?"

"Ten days," Carlotta corrected lightly, leaning against the desk in her home office. She extended her left hand to stare at her sparkling engagement ring. "We're not kids anymore, we don't want to wait. The invitations went out yesterday."

Dressed in a black romper and combat boots, Hannah looked dubious. "You're not pregnant, are you?"

"No."

Hannah patted her own rounded stomach. "Too bad—our tots could grow up together."

Carlotta smiled. "I can't wait to see you be a mom."

"Ugh, don't wish away the last few months of my freedom." Hannah bit into her lip. "Are you sure you're ready for this?"

"I will be," Carlotta said. "I've thought about my wedding day since I was a little girl—it's going to be *perfect*."

"I was talking about the marriage."

Carlotta frowned. "The pregnant woman who doesn't live with her husband is giving out marital advice?"

"Long-distance marriages aren't new—look at all the couples who survive being separated by war."

"Your husband isn't away at war. He's across town working at my dad's driving range." Carlotta angled her head. "You still haven't told your parents you're married, have you?"

Hannah scowled. "It's your fault. I was planning to finally break the news last weekend, but my dad found out I asked an employee at the Dallas hotel to send me the security footage the night Patricia Alexander died, and he almost blew a damn gasket."

Carlotta's shoulders fell. "Oh. Sorry."

"I'm just glad you've moved past Patricia's death," Hannah said in a soothing voice. "And now you have the wedding to keep you occupied."

"Right." Carlotta's gaze strayed to an easel that held a whiteboard she'd hastily covered with a black Burberry scarf when Hannah arrived.

"But you'll be happy to know," Hannah continued, "I plan to introduce Chance to my parents this evening over dinner at one of my dad's restaurants."

"As your husband?"

"Um… I thought I'd introduce him first as a friend, and as the alcohol flows, ease into the fact that he's the father of my child, and by dessert, hopefully my folks will be smashed enough for me to drop the bomb that we're married."

"They haven't asked about the baby's father?"

"No."

Carlotta angled her head again. "You haven't told them about the baby, have you?"

"I wanted to get my story straight. And actually, this is perfect timing—they'll be so happy about the baby, they'll overlook the fact that Chance isn't exactly what they hoped for in a son-in-law."

"He's not a bad guy," Carlotta murmured, feeling compelled to defend her friend's choice in a spouse. But recalling all the times Chance had involved Wesley in criminal activity, she squelched the impulse to add "anymore."

"He's trying to be better," Hannah said earnestly. "And now that my mukbang business is taking off, he's been able to let go of some of his shadier side hustles."

Carlotta shook her head. "I can't believe you're making a living eating in front of an online audience."

"Ain't the Internet great?" She pounded on her breastbone and released a belch. "But between the baby and all the performance food, I have air coming out both ends all the damn time. Luckily, burping and farting during and after eating a big meal is considered good form in some countries."

"Luckily," Carlotta agreed wryly.

"How's your business?" Hannah asked, gesturing around the room Wesley had transformed from their parents' old bedroom into a spacious office for her with desk, bookcases, and work surfaces on one side, and upholstered seating grouped around a long table on the other side. Overflowing racks of colorful clothing lined the perimeter. In the corner a mounted TV screen was tuned to the Style channel.

"Better than I could've hoped after the social media frenzy with the Kenzie Jamison emoji jeans." Carlotta nodded to the wall where a pair of the infamously viral blue jeans had been mounted in a glass shadow box.

"You single-handedly saved that celebrity's clothing line."

"The credit goes to the factory girl in Tennessee who was clever enough to cover a mistake with the emoji patch... I simply found a pair of the jeans and started posting about them."

"And made them famous," Hannah added. "How much are those dungarees worth?"

"The last I checked, pairs from the original line of ten thousand were going for almost five grand a piece."

"Unbelievable. And how much did you make brokering them?"

Carlotta grinned. "Enough to pad my bank account until I can get my business rolling." She reached around and plucked a white card from an open box, then handed it to Hannah. "While I was at the printer getting the wedding invitations, I sprang for new business cards."

"Carlotta's Closet," Hannah read. "Personal shopper and brand representative. Wow, that's so... *you*."

"I have a dozen clients so far," Carlotta said, unable to contain her enthusiasm. Then she stopped. "Which means I can't go on the nursing home body runs anymore."

"I can't do them by myself!"

"I'm sorry. But you're going to have to retire soon anyway. You can't pick up bodies for the morgue with a Baby on Board sign in the window of the van."

Hannah pouted and stomped her foot. "I feel like things are *changing*."

"They are," Carlotta said with a little smile. "For the better... for all of us."

Hannah gave a begrudged nod. "I'm happy for you and Coop. I know he's over the moon. How did Detective Dickhead take it?"

Carlotta gave a little shrug. "I don't know. I haven't seen Jack since Walt Tully was taken into custody."

"I hope he gave you credit for that takedown," Hannah said dryly.

"Since he saved me from drowning after Walt pushed me off the marina dock, he probably considers us even."

Her friend harrumphed. "Have you run into Tracey since her father was arrested?"

Carlotta wet her lips carefully. She was still smarting over the revelation from a DNA family tree program that Tracey was her half-sister, which meant Walt Tully, the man who'd engineered the Ponzi and counterfeiting scheme that had taken down the firm of Mashburn & Tully and the fortunes of many innocent people along with it, and whom she suspected had ordered the hit on Peter Ashford in lockup, was her biological father. "No. I'm sure Tracey hates me for revealing she was hiding Walt at her houseboat."

"Hasn't she always hated you anyway?"

Carlotta nodded. "I feel for her, though—she was protecting her father, and I've been in her shoes."

"Except Randolph was innocent of what he was accused of."

"But there was a time when I believed he was guilty, and still I felt obligated to protect him."

Hannah sighed. "Family... what an ass-ache. Speaking of, how's Wes?"

Carlotta's heart lifted and she smiled. "He's at the airport, waiting for Meg to arrive."

"That girl is one lucky backpacker."

"You're so right. Apparently the people who kidnapped her in Ireland intended to transport her to Russia for... I can't even say it."

"Sex slavery," Hannah said flatly. "Fuckers deserve to die screaming."

"Can't argue there, but something happened to change their plan. She was dropped off at the hotel where her father was staying, and the person who did it disappeared."

"A happy ending—that doesn't happen often."

"I don't know," Carlotta said with a little laugh. "You got yours."

"Talk to me after I introduce my husband to my dad." Hannah checked the chunky watch on her wrist. "Gotta run... I need to squeeze in a mukbang before tonight's come-clean dinner."

When Hannah wheeled toward the door, the movement displaced the scarf covering the whiteboard. It slid to the floor, revealing photos and a diagram of arrows. Carlotta rushed to block her friend's view, but was too late.

"What's all this?" Hannah asked, her voice undulating with suspicion. She studied the photos—one of Patricia Alexander and Carlotta together at the Wedding World Expo, and several from the scene of Patricia's death, the Dallas hotel bathroom, plus one of a redheaded woman—along with images cut from a magazine, and hand-drawn arrows connecting the images to a timeline. Hannah turned her questioning gaze to Carlotta. "I thought you'd accepted Patricia's death was an accident."

Carlotta lifted her chin. "I learned some new information."

Hannah closed her eyes briefly. "What new information?"

Carlotta pointed to the picture of the redhead. "This is Colleen Mason."

"Why is her name familiar to me?"

"She's the woman who claimed she had an affair with Senator Max Reeder."

"Oh, right. Wait—didn't she commit suicide?"

"Allegedly."

Hannah squinted. "What does she have to do with Patricia?"

Carlotta pointed to the woman's photo. "The black makeup case she's carrying in this photo is the same makeup case Patricia had. It's unique, and expensive."

"Okay."

"And Colleen Mason was on our flight to Dallas."

"I'm not following."

"Before she died, Colleen Mason claimed to have proof of her affair with the Senator."

"Right. Everyone assumed she had some version of a blue dress with a stain, like Monica Lewinsky."

Carlotta pointed to a photo she'd taken of the baggie she'd found behind the waste basket in Patricia's hotel bathroom. "What if the proof was a used condom?"

Hannah's eyes bugged. "You think the condom belonged to the Senator?"

"Maybe."

"I'm trying to connect the dots. *How* did it get in Patricia's bathroom?"

"There was an... incident on the plane." Carlotta's face grew warm. "Patricia and I had words and passengers complained. The flight attendant made us get off the plane first."

Hannah guffawed.

Carlotta ignored her. "What if when Patricia removed her makeup case from the overhead bin, she accidentally took Colleen Mason's bag?"

"And the condom was in the bag?"

"That's what I'm thinking." Carlotta pointed to photos of the bathroom vanity. "When I studied these before, something bothered me, but I couldn't put my finger on it. But look at the products all over counter, like they were spilled. And there are lots of different brands, all inexpensive. But look at the open makeup case—it's full of carefully arranged matching products, all brands that Neiman's carries. I think *this* is Patricia's makeup case."

"And the other products came from Colleen Mason's bag."

"There's no room in the makeup bag in the picture for the products that are scattered all over."

Hannah shook her head as if she was trying to absorb all the information. "You think someone killed Patricia because she picked up the wrong dang makeup bag?"

Carlotta lifted her shoulders in a slow shrug. "People have killed over less. Maybe Colleen Mason went to Patricia's hotel room to swap out the bag and they argued."

"How would the Mason woman have known where to find Patricia?"

Carlotta pointed to a box on the whiteboard where she'd written 'Trevor Biondi.' "The taxi valet flirted with Patricia—he got her business card, and knew where we were staying. Maybe Colleen Mason told him Patricia had her bag, and he gave her the name of the hotel."

"Do you still have the condom?"

"It's in the freezer." Carlotta smiled. "It makes sense, right?"

Hannah blinked twice... three times. "It makes more sense that Patricia was foggy from the meds she was taking, fell in the hotel bathroom and hit her head on the tile floor and died, like the police said, and like Coop said. And the condom was discarded by who knows what hotel guest who stayed in that room before Patricia."

Carlotta drooped.

"You see that, don't you?" Hannah asked carefully.

"So, I shouldn't present this theory to Jack?"

"No, you definitely should. Because he'll stroke out and then you can marry Coop with no interference."

Carlotta scoffed. "Jack isn't going to interfere with the wedding. He's happy for me and Coop."

"Uh-huh." Hannah sighed. "Look, you're obviously not done with Patricia's death. I get it, you feel guilty because we made fun of her quirks. But are you sure you're not dwelling on this to distract you from the fact that you're getting fucking married?"

Carlotta pressed her lips together, hard. "I'm *sure*. And speaking of the wedding... will you be my Maid of Honor?"

Hannah's face split into a wide grin. "I thought you'd never ask... fuck yeah!" She clasped Carlotta in a bear hug and rocked her back and forth.

"Promise me you'll clean up your language when the baby gets here," Carlotta murmured.

"I fucking promise. Shit damn, you're getting married."

Carlotta laughed. "I'm getting married."

CHAPTER 2

WESLEY'S LEG jumped uncontrollably. He leaned forward in his chair and glanced at the clock on the wall of the private lounge in the Atlanta airport. "Shouldn't the plane have landed by now?"

Detective Jack Terry swung his head toward him. "Why don't you and I go get something to drink?"

"I don't want anything to drink."

"Come with me anyway."

The big man pushed to his feet, then addressed Meg's mother who sat nearby with a friend, both of them wearing concerned expressions. "Can we bring you ladies coffee, or maybe tea?"

They smiled and agreed coffee would be nice.

Wes stood and followed Jack, feeling disgruntled. "Why is the plane late?"

Jack leveled his gaze on him. "Relax, Wes. You're making Mrs. Vincent nervous. The plane will get here when it gets here."

Wes tightened his mouth, then pushed up his glasses. "Why are you here again?"

"I told you—to debrief Meg when she arrives so the GBI can close the case."

Wes wiped a hand over his suddenly moist neck. When Meg had called him from Ireland, she'd divulged the name she'd overheard of her rescuer—Birch. Randolph's right hand man, babysitter, and bodyguard. While Wesley had been hating his dad for doing everything in his power to keep Wes from running off to Europe and violating his probation, Randolph had sent Birch, the man with the mysterious background, to handle the international situation. When he'd asked his dad to explain, Randolph had extracted a promise from him and from Meg to play dumb.

But would Meg buckle under Jack Terry's questioning?

"So Meg is your girlfriend, huh?'

Wes lifted his head, then gave a little shrug. "Yeah... I think."

"You don't know?"

Wes frowned. "I know. Meg and I are... together."

Jack stopped at the coffee station and began to fill four cups. "You couldn't dress up a little?"

Wes glanced down at his shabby jeans and loose-fitting T-shirt and panicked—he looked like a slob. His mouth tightened. "I don't need to impress Meg."

"Good thing," Jack drawled.

What a dick. "Carlotta's engaged," he blurted.

Jack didn't react, but a muscle worked in his jaw. "Coop told me."

"You're okay with that?"

Jack lifted one of the cups for a drink, then winced. "Why wouldn't I be? It's Carlotta's life, and she's been engaged before."

"They set a date."

"Yeah, Coop invited me."

Wes snorted. "Surely you said no."

Jack added cream to each of the coffees. "So who's the guy who flew over with Meg's dad?"

Wes swallowed the sour taste in his mouth. "Friend of her dead brother. Mark likes Meg, but he's a preppy kiss-ass."

Jack handed two of the coffees to Wes. "Still, you'd better watch your back."

"Or I'll end up like you?"

Jack scowled. "Drink your coffee, smartass."

Wes enjoyed goading the cocky man because out of the three men who'd been vying for his sister's attention, he preferred Coop.

He just hoped Carlotta preferred Coop, too.

Meg's mother looked up as they approached, her expression animated. "Harold just texted me—they've landed. He and Mark will bring Meg here as soon as they deplane."

Wes's heart rate spiked—she was close. He reclaimed his seat and downed the coffee in record time. Now his leg was really jumping.

"Easy," Jack murmured for his ears only.

"You're right, I should've dressed up."

"Too late now."

"And I should've brought her some flowers. Girls like that stuff."

"Yep."

Wes frowned. "Thanks for the moral support."

Jack grunted "If not for the bracelet you gave her, Meg might've not been reported missing for days or weeks longer. Remember that."

Wes gave a curt nod, and exhaled. "What are you going to ask Meg?"

"If she's remembered any details since she was dropped off at her father's hotel, anything that might help track down the people who kidnapped her, or the people who returned her."

Wes moistened his lips. "You don't think it was the same people?"

Jack shrugged. "Maybe, maybe not. It doesn't make sense to me that the traffickers suddenly grew a conscience. I could more easily believe that somebody else was involved."

"Somebody else?" Wes parroted in a squeaky voice. "Who?"

"I don't know... someone with a vested interest in getting Meg home. Her father is wealthy, influential. Maybe he has friends in high places who can make things happen."

Wes's mouth watered to say it was *his* dad who'd made things happen, but he'd promised Randolph he'd stay quiet.

"Or maybe this friend of hers, Mark. Is he well off?"

"Probably," Wes said bitterly. "But he's a wuss."

"Maybe, but money talks, especially in criminal circles."

Wes scoffed. "Dude, I can one hundred percent guarantee that Marky Mark had nothing to do with Meg being rescued."

Jack's eyebrows shot up. "Really?"

Realizing his gaffe, Wes back-pedaled. "I mean... he's not that smart."

The door to the lounge opened and Wes sat forward. A man entered, carrying an enormous bouquet of flowers and balloons. "Delivery for Meg from Mark, can someone sign?"

While Meg's mother signed for the delivery, Jack gave Wes a pointed look.

"Shut up," Wes muttered, more nervous than ever that Mark had somehow managed to insinuate himself into Meg's heart as she'd recovered. When she'd first called Wes, she'd said "I love you," but emotions had been running high... what if she'd changed her mind?

Damn all the coffee, now he had to piss like a racehorse, but he didn't want to miss Meg's arrival. He squirmed in his seat until Meg's mother asked if he was alright. Wes excused himself and jogged to the men's room, cursing Jack and his coffee. He drained his bladder as quickly as he could, but had to wait for another guy to finish at the sink before he could wash his hands. When he ran out of the bathroom, the Vincents, Meg, Mark, and the family friend were embracing, laughing and crying.

He'd missed it.

Meg's honey-colored hair was longer, and she looked thinner. She was wearing a loose flowered dress, and pink tennis shoes. He edged closer, hoping Meg would notice him, feeling like an interloper.

Jack spotted him. "And here's Wes," he announced.

Meg extracted herself from her mother's arms, grinned, and ran to him. His heart buoyed high as he caught her and wrapped her in a hug as tightly as he dared. She felt fragile. He wanted to never let her go. "Mm," he murmured into her ear. "Mm." He didn't trust himself to speak, could only hold her close and try to soak her in.

Across the room, Dr. Vincent cleared his throat loudly. "Meg, sweetheart, Detective Terry would like a word, then we can take you home so you can rest... in private."

The last two words seemed aimed at him, considering Dr. Vincent was stabbing him with knife eyes.

Jack walked toward them, giving Wes a rueful glance. "We can talk over here, Meg, where it's quiet. I'll be brief so you can be with... your loved ones."

When they pulled apart, Wes tried to make eye contact with her, to warn her again not to mention Birch, but he wasn't sure if she understood. "I want to listen in," Wes said.

Jack frowned. "This is police business."

"But you said if not for the bracelet I gave Meg—"

"Fine," Jack cut in, then waved them toward a cubicle designed for the traveling professional.

"I want to listen in, too," Mark said, walking toward them, holding the flowers and balloons he'd had delivered.

"Sorry." Jack held up his hand. "No more room."

Wes grudgingly acknowledged Jack had done him a solid, although it was more likely the man simply wanted to cut to the chase and close the case file. There were only two chairs. After Meg lowered herself into one, Wes let Jack have the other one. He positioned himself behind Jack so he could signal Meg if necessary.

"Welcome home," Jack said to Meg.

"Thank you," she said, looking tentative.

"I'm Detective Terry with the Atlanta Police Department. I also liaise with the GBI, which is why I was on your case. I just need a few more details before we close the file."

"Okay," Meg said.

"What can you tell me about the day you were returned to the hotel where your father was staying?"

She glanced at Wes and looked a little panicked. Wes shook his head slightly.

Jack must've noticed her distraction because he turned around to glance at Wes.

Wes schooled his face into nonchalance. "You don't have to be nervous, Meg. Jack looks like an asshole, but inside he's a big teddy bear."

Jack scowled at him. "Quiet." Then he turned back to Meg. "Go ahead, Ms. Vincent."

"I told this story to the local police the day I was dropped off."

"I know, but sometimes things get lost in translation between different police departments, so I'd rather hear it from you."

She glanced at Wes again. He telegraphed to give the man something.

"I... don't remember much," she said carefully. "I was being held in a hotel room. A man and a woman were watching me. They gave me sleeping pills, so I was in and out of consciousness. I remember a man waking me up and when I couldn't walk, he carried me out. I thought he was one of my captors and I resisted as much as I could, but he finally convinced me he was there to take me home."

"And what do you remember about this man?"

She bounced another look to Wesley, then lifted her shoulders in a slow shrug. "Not much."

"Can you describe him?"

"Um... not really... it was nighttime when we were driving, and for most of that time I was asleep in the backseat."

"Did he tell you his name, or say anything distinctive?"

"No," she said in a high voice.

"Hm... according to the police report, you said you overheard the name 'Beith' spelled B-E-I-T-H?"

Wes relaxed... the Irish police had misunderstood the name.

Meg swallowed, then shook her head. "I don't remember saying that."

"The man didn't talk at all?"

"Um... he said I'd be back home in Atlanta before I knew it."

Jack's shoulders straightened. "He was American?"

Meg looked panicked. "I, uh... that is... I don't know."

"Did he speak English with an American accent?"

"I... can't remember. I was pretty fuzzy from the drugs."

Jack shifted on the chair. "I'm just wondering how he knew you were from Atlanta."

Meg shot a wide-eyed look to Wes.

"It was all over the news," Wes offered. "Everyone knew a girl from Atlanta had gone missing."

"That must be it," Meg said, visibly relieved.

"Okay," Jack said, nodding. "We're just trying to determine if this guy was part of the kidnapping crew, or some kind of Good Samaritan."

"Does it matter?" Wes asked.

Jack turned, then gave them both a flat smile. "I guess it doesn't. What's important is you're back with your family."

Meg gave him a watery smile.

"So we're done here?" Wes asked.

Jack hesitated, then nodded. "We're done. Again, welcome home, Ms. Vincent."

"Thank you," she murmured.

Wes studiously avoided making eye contact with Jack as they left the cubicle. At the other end of the lounge, Meg's parents, family friend, and Mark stood near the exit, waiting. Meg's mother opened her arms to envelope her daughter into another hug.

"Let's get you home," Dr. Vincent said.

The group left the lounge. Wes walked with them, but as they approached the airport exit, it was clear they were circling the wagons around Meg and excluding him. He fell back to walk next to Jack. At the exit, Meg turned.

"Wes, you can come home with us."

"Uh, no," her father said. "There won't be room. Mark left his car at the house, so he needs a ride."

Mark shot Wes a "sorry-not sorry" look. Wes had to bite his tongue not to say there'd be plenty of room if they left the obnoxious bouquet of flowers and balloons behind.

"That's okay," Wes said to Meg. "I'll come visit later."

"Meg needs to rest," Dr. Vincent said pointedly. "She won't be having visitors for a while." The man's gaze dropped to Wes's ankle.

Wes looked down to see his pants leg had ridden up, revealing his court-ordered GPS monitoring device. He'd been dinged for removing it when he'd been on the verge of taking off for Europe, so he had to wear it for a while longer. Hot frustration rose in his chest.

Meg looked torn, then gave Wes a little smile. "I'll call you."

He nodded and maintained his smile until they'd disappeared through the automatic sliding doors. Then he muttered a foul word.

"They need time," Jack offered.

"Who asked you?" Wes shot back.

"Right. Give you a ride home?"

Wes turned in the opposite direction. "Nope," he said over his shoulder. "I'd rather take the train."

CHAPTER 3

CARLOTTA STARED at her reflection in the mirror, trying to whip up enthusiasm for the white georgette wedding gown with satin corset.

"Are you coming out?" her younger sister Prissy called, sounding tired.

Carlotta pushed aside the curtain of the Neiman Marcus dressing room, gathered up the full skirt, and stepped out. Her audience—her mother, Prissy, and Hannah—straightened and gave her hopeful smiles.

"It's lovely," Valerie said.

"So pretty," Prissy seconded.

"My favorite so far," Hannah added, suppressing a yawn.

"But what do *you* think?" her mother asked.

Carlotta turned and viewed the dress from all angles in a three-way mirror. "I love the fabric, and I thought this dress would be *the* one."

The spectators sagged. They'd been patient as she'd tried on several racks of gowns—A-line, mermaid, backless, sheath, mini, midi, lace, chiffon, organza, satin, silk, plunging neckline, boat neck, keyhole, sweetheart, sleeveless, puff sleeves, off one shoulder...

"But?" her mother prompted.

"But... I don't know, it just doesn't *feel* right."

"Maybe you should reconsider wearing white," Hannah said dryly.

Carlotta sent a frown toward her friend. "I'm sorry it's taking so long, but I want my wedding dress to be perfect."

"Of course you do," Valerie soothed. "You'll find it."

"But you'll have to try another store," Prissy pointed out, "since you've tried on everything here."

Carlotta surveyed the drooping threesome. "Why don't we call it a day, we're all getting tired. I'll try again another time."

"Good idea," Hannah said, pushing to her feet. "Next time I'll wear a diaper."

"At least we found *our* dresses," Prissy said, holding up the pale pink princess dress she'd be wearing as the flower girl.

"Yes," Valerie said, nodding to the paler pink mother-of-the-bride lace dress hanging nearby. "I love mine."

"I can't believe you're making me wear pink," Hannah groused, picking up the babydoll dress she'd set aside.

"The color is shell," Carlotta argued. "And you know it looks terrific on you."

"And it'll still fit your baby bump when the wedding gets here," Prissy added with a grin.

Hannah sighed. "I'm only wearing it to make you happy, Miss Priss. I gotta run."

"Are you mukbanging today?" Prissy asked.

"You know it," Hannah said. "I'm trending, can't let down my fans." She walked up next to Carlotta and leaned in. "You seem distracted."

"I'm not." Then Carlotta sighed. "Okay, maybe I am... a little."

"You're thinking about Patricia, aren't you?"

"It's like she's haunting me."

"Let it *go*, Carlotta. Let Patricia rest in peace."

"I'm trying," Carlotta said earnestly. "Hey—how did it go when you introduced Chance to your parents?"

"It was a disaster. He was nervous, and high. He offered my dad a hit of Molly. They kind of hate him."

Carlotta winced. "I'm sorry. They must be happy about the baby, though."

"We didn't get that far. When I told them Chance and I were dating—"

"Dating?"

"I was planning to ease into the whole marriage thing, then slip in the fact that Chance and I had procreated, but they left the restaurant before the appetizers arrived." Hannah sighed. "My dad has high expectations for my coupling."

"Most fathers do."

"You're so lucky that your folks love Coop."

Carlotta nodded. "I know. But your parents will warm up to Chance in time."

Hannah pointed to her stomach. "I have five months for Chance to morph into a respectable businessman."

That seemed like a stretch goal for any amount of time, but instead of voicing her concern, Carlotta gave her friend a bolstering smile. "Or you could tell your folks that the heart wants what it wants."

Hannah considered her advice. "Nah. I'm banking on a miracle." She waved goodbye to Valerie and Prissy, then marched away.

Carlotta shook her head, then looked back to her reflection and suppressed a shudder. "Ugh. I can't believe I thought this dress would work."

Valerie walked up and made eye contact with Carlotta in the mirror. "Prissy, stay with our dresses. I'm going to help your sister with the zipper. It looks tricky."

Carlotta dutifully lifted the voluminous skirt and walked back into the dressing room. Her mother followed and stepped in behind her. "Is everything okay? You seem preoccupied."

Carlotta's mind spun. Valerie would be horrified if she knew Carlotta had learned the identity of her biological father, and worried if she thought Carlotta was still fixated on Patricia's cause of death.

"Everything's fine." She offered a smile to her mother's concerned expression. "I'm engaged to a wonderful man, Wes's girlfriend is home safe and he's staying out of trouble. My business is getting off the ground, you're going gangbusters with the StyleMe Hanger—I can't remember when things were this good."

Valerie lowered the zipper and helped Carlotta step out of the gown. "You're not still brooding over the locket I gave you?" Her tone was light, but obviously she'd been giving the heavy subject some thought.

Carlotta turned and clasped her mother's hands. "No. I love Dad, he'll always be my dad. I want him to walk me down the aisle."

Her mother brightened. "Good. He'll love that, too—well, not the giving away part, but he knows you'll be happy with Coop."

"Of course I will be."

"So… nothing's worrying you about the wedding?"

Carlotta scoffed. "The only thing that's worrying me about the wedding is whether I'll find the right dress."

"You will." Valerie checked her watch. "I'm sorry, but I do have to get Prissy to an after-school thing. Let us know when you want to do this again."

"Okay, Mom… thanks."

They embraced and Valerie slipped out. Carlotta waited until she was sure they were gone before she closed her eyes and heaved a heavy sigh. She wanted to be deliriously obsessed with her wedding, but she couldn't be as long as so many questions were left unanswered about Patricia's death. Trying on gowns only reminded her of the week she'd spent with Patricia at the World Wedding Expo. While they hadn't become best buds, she'd come to understand what motivated the woman and admire her pluckiness. It still seemed preposterous that Patricia was gone, and the thought that she might've been killed over something so frivolous as a swapped makeup case left Carlotta breathless with grief.

She gave herself a mental shake, then dressed in her street clothes and stopped to thank the sales associate who'd made the bridal department available to Carlotta for a private fitting session.

"Lindy Russell asked us to give you the white-glove treatment," the young woman said. "You're sales royalty around here, Carlotta."

"That's kind of you to say," Carlotta murmured. She missed the bustle of the retail environment, but she was excited to be starting something new. On the way out of the store, she stopped by Lindy's office to say hello and to drop off a few business cards. Her former boss seemed pleased to see her.

"We miss you around here," Lindy said, then her expression turned circumspect. "Retail is more challenging than ever, we've had to cut staff. But I floated the idea of working with freelance personal shoppers like you by senior management, and they're intrigued. If you're willing, I might use you as a case study."

"That'd be great," Carlotta said. "Call me anytime."

She left the mall feeling a little lighter, but on the train ride home, her mind turned back to the DNA sample in her freezer. What if her theory was right, that it belonged to Senator Max Reeder and Patricia had been killed for it, and she did nothing?

When she got off the train, her feet carried her to the hotel where she'd previously used the business center to access the results of her own DNA and the DNA in the baggie. When she'd seen the DNA hadn't matched the genetic profile of either of the two men she'd suspected might have murdered Patricia, she'd let it go. It hadn't occurred to her to pay the extra fee and see if the DNA donor had relatives registered in the worldwide family tree because she'd dismissed the idea the sample had something to do with Patricia's death. But with her new theory…

Carlotta lowered her sunglasses and strolled into the lobby of the hotel as if she were a guest. The large shoulder bag could pass as luggage. Besides, she'd learned a long time ago crashing parties that if a person acted as if they belonged somewhere, they were unlikely to be questioned. She knew her way to the business center on the mezzanine where she claimed one of the public computers made available to guests. With a few clicks she accessed the email of the address she'd made up, and clicked on the original email providing the genetic makeup of the sample. At the bottom of the email she was given the option to *Add your genetic profile to the worldwide family tree to see if you have DNA matches.*

She clicked on the link and, mindful of not having the DNA entry tied back to her, paid the fee with a debit gift card she'd bought with cash. Adrenaline pumped through her veins as she waited for the results. If the profile linked to the Reeder family, she would have enough evidence to go to Jack.

In a few seconds, the results scrolled onto the screen:
Matches in Parent/Child: 0

Matches in Immediate Family (full siblings, grandparents, or grandchildren): 0

Matches in Close Family (aunt or an uncle, niece or nephew, half-sibling): 0

Her disappointment was acute. On one hand it seemed likely a family with a deep southern lineage like the Reeders would have registered profiles... on the other hand some political figures might think there were too many skeletons in the closet to risk it.

Especially politicians vying for their party's nomination for President.

A groan of frustration vibrated in her throat.

Her own DNA profile and "leaf" on the tree stirred up unsettling thoughts. An irresistible compulsion rose to double-check the results. She accessed email for the alternate address she'd set up, then stopped.

At the top of the inbox was a message from TraceyTLowenstein.

Her heart nearly leapt out of her chest before she realized Tracey couldn't know who she'd reached out to—the email address Carlotta had generated to register the kit was a series of jumbled letters.

Still, her pulse raced as she clicked on the note.

Hello, I noticed you and I are matched in the worldwide family tree as "aunt, uncle, niece, nephew, or half-sibling." I live in Atlanta, Georgia, USA, and would like to know more about you. I hope you will respond and let me know how we are related. Tracey

Carlotta's breath caught in her chest, and her face flooded with heat as she contemplated hitting the Reply button. Didn't Tracey deserve to know? Her mind fast-forwarded to the ramifications to all parties—betrayal, heartache, estrangement. All for a chance to connect with a half-sister who already despised her.

She clicked off the note and fumbled to close the window and the session, then hastily backtracked through the hotel lobby. By the time she reached the sidewalk, she was jogging, trying to outrun the inconvenient truth.

CHAPTER 4

"FOR DAILY tableware, do you prefer the Greystone pattern or the Juniper?" Carlotta held up two plates for Coop to study.

He squinted. "Am I allowed to say either one?"

"You don't have a preference?"

Coop smiled. "I do not." He glanced around the housewares department of Neiman's and puffed out his cheeks. "In fact, everything here looks nice to me. I trust your judgement entirely when it comes to the gift registry."

She bit into her lip. "I like the Juniper pattern, but it's kind of pricey."

He shrugged. "You only get married once."

She grinned. "Hopefully." Then she pursed her mouth. "But since we're not registering fine china, maybe it's okay to choose the more expensive day dishes."

"That makes sense to me."

"You're bored, aren't you?"

"No," he said quickly. "I'm never bored when I'm with you." He came up behind her to nuzzle her neck. "I'm just more focused on the honeymoon than the gift registry."

She laughed, rolling her neck from the chills his mouth sent over her shoulders. "If I drop these plates they'll make us leave."

"Promise?"

"Coop! We have a lot to do in a short period of time. Did you make reservations for your parents at the hotel?"

"Yes. They can't wait to meet you."

"Do you think I'm what they expect?"

He laughed. "No. You're much more. They're going to love you as much as I do."

She warmed. "My parents adore you, too… and Wes. He's so happy to be working at the morgue with you."

"It's not charity—I'm happy to have someone I can rely on."

"And now that Meg is home safe, I'm starting to feel as if Wes might be okay." She sighed. "Although I still worry about his relationship with Randolph."

"Fathers and sons are tough. My dad and I had some rough times, too."

"I can't imagine you being a difficult child."

"Difficult in that I was different from him," Coop said. "My dad is a mechanical engineer, was really into cars and working with his hands. I had more of a mind for biology, and was close to my uncle, my mother's brother."

"The one who owns Motherwell's Funeral Home?"

"Right."

"But you obviously got your love of cars from your dad."

He grinned. "Yeah. I found my way, and my dad and I are close now. Wes will do the same. By the way, I thought I'd ask him to be a groomsman—do you think he'll be okay with that?"

"I think he'll be thrilled," Carlotta said. "I asked Hannah to be my Maid of Honor, and Prissy to be our flower girl."

"I thought you might," Coop said, nodding.

"Have you chosen your Best Man?"

He coughed. "I, uh, asked Jack."

Carlotta blinked. "Jack?" Surprise shot through her, but she scrambled to recover. "And what did he say?"

"He said yes." Coop angled his head. "Should I have asked you first? Will it be awkward?"

"No," she said quickly. "Jack and I are… friends. And I know you two go way back… long before I was on the scene."

"We do, and although we've had our differences, Jack always had my back. And I can't blame him for being attracted to you." Then he winked. "Besides, it's better to keep your rivals close."

She gave him a withering look.

His phone buzzed. He pulled it out to check the screen, then grunted. "I hate to do this, but I'm going to have to leave the rest of the gift registry in your capable hands."

She made a face. "Are you sure you didn't text yourself to get out of this?"

He laughed. "Call you later?"

"Please," she said, then abandoned the plates to loop her arms around his neck.

His eyes smiled into hers. "I can't wait until you're my wife." He clasped her mouth in a warm, wet kiss, then pulled away reluctantly.

Carlotta watched him stride away. Tall and lean, he moved with casual confidence. Coop was smart and sexy... and he was going to be her husband.

Husband.

The more she said the word, the more nonsensical it sounded. But then, weren't all the activities leading up to the wedding for the purpose of getting accustomed to the idea of having a spouse?

She glanced around the housewares department and suddenly felt overwhelmed at the thought of choosing flatware, glassware, and pots and pans by herself—especially since the kitchen wasn't exactly her domain. She'd come back another day. After tucking the registry printout into her bag, she headed toward the nearest exit.

And although she'd told Coop she was fine with Jack serving as their Best Man, the news was a little jarring. Everyone in their immediate circle was aware of her rollercoaster involvement with Jack... on the other hand, maybe this was both men's way of publicly acknowledging their place in her life.

Maybe it would give them all closure.

She left the mall and walked to the lot where she'd parked her white Miata convertible. Just the sight of it made her smile. Randolph had given it to her for her sixteenth birthday, an indulgence the Wrens could afford at the time. But a mere two years after, her parents were on the lam and she was struggling to pay for gasoline. When the car had broken down, it had sat in the garage at the townhouse for years because she couldn't afford to get it repaired, yet neither did she want to sell what felt like the last tangible connection to her missing father. When the Wren family reunited, Randolph had been touched that she'd kept the Miata. But when she'd recently learned that Randolph wasn't her biological father, one of her impulsive responses was to allow Coop to repair the convertible with the thought of selling it. Thankfully, though, she'd come to terms with the fact that biology be damned—Randolph was her father. Now the joy of driving the convertible outpaced even the pleasure of when she'd first driven it because the meaning of the gift had come full circle.

When she pulled the car to the exit of the mall parking lot, she hesitated a few seconds before turning toward the midtown police precinct where Jack was based. She would tell him what she'd learned about Patricia's case. Hopefully he'd agree the circumstances were too coincidental to ignore. Then she could leave the investigation to him and focus on her wedding.

Although there was another outstanding issue…

She pulled up Rainie Stephens's number and connected the call.

The investigative reporter for the *Atlanta Journal-Constitution* answered on the first ring. "Hi, Carlotta, what's up?"

"Hi, Rainie. Just wondering if your sources at the jail have heard any more rumors about who might've targeted Peter Ashford."

"I'm not supposed to talk to you, police orders."

Carlotta frowned. "Jack Terry?"

"Uh huh. But between you and me, my informant hasn't heard anything new."

"Can you push him a little? Now that Walt Tully is locked up, maybe he's talking."

Rainie sighed. "I can't make any promises."

"Thanks, Rainie."

"Oh, hey—I got your wedding invitation. Wow, you and Coop aren't wasting any time."

Carlotta bit into her lip. "I hope this isn't awkward. We both want you to come… we'd like to meet your fiancé."

"I'll be there," Rainie said. "You and I should get together sometime and compare wedding planning notes. Who knew it was this much work?"

"Right," Carlotta said, pushing aside guilt over all she wasn't getting done. "Absolutely, let's get together soon."

She ended the call just as the building that housed the police precinct came into view. She maneuvered the little car into an empty spot, then decided to text Jack to see if he was available— and in a decent mood—instead of ambushing him this late in the afternoon.

Hi, Jack... I'm around the corner. Do you have time to talk?

A few seconds later her phone buzzed.

I have 10 minutes.

She frowned and considered postponing the talk because he obviously wasn't in a good temper... although she'd probably have to wait forever to catch the man in a jolly mood.

She flipped down the visor to stroke on lipstick—her secret weapon for increasing the chances that a man like Jack Terry would pay attention to what was coming out of her mouth.

After pressing a button to raise the top of the convertible for security, she walked into the building, registering the fact that she was far too familiar with local, state, and federal incarceration facilities around Atlanta.

Opting for the stairs, she climbed to the floor that housed the bustling office. When she walked into the raucous waiting room, she was swept back to the day when she'd first come here after receiving a slightly terrifying call from Wes that he'd been arrested. She'd arrived in a flop sweat to clash with Detective Terry who'd arrested him and who would later reopen her father's case.

Shortly after she'd been reunited with Peter Ashford, her first love, and met Wes's new boss, Cooper Craft. The three men would change her life forever.

At the thought of Peter, her heart squeezed painfully. She would never get used to the idea that he was gone forever. It seemed incomprehensible that life had simply marched on since he'd been killed in jail by another inmate. Indeed, she nursed guilty pangs for planning such a happy event on the heels of his death.

She hadn't forgotten her promise at his grave to find whoever was responsible and make them pay. But that was before she realized the man she suspected had ordered Peter's death was her biological father.

The waiting room of the midtown police precinct was a teeming cross-section of Atlanta humanity, every gender, skin color, and socio-economic class seemed to be represented. Some people looked defiant, some scared, and some bored. Corralling everyone from behind a panel of bullet-proof glass was a no-nonsense woman named Brooklyn. Carlotta stood in the rear, waiting her turn at the window. When Brooklyn next scanned the area, her eyes stopped on Carlotta and her face split in a grin. She lifted her hand and gestured for Carlotta to come forward.

Carlotta threaded her way through pressing bodies, murmuring pardons. At last she leaned into the window. "Hi, Brook. I came to see Jack. He's expecting me."

The woman's gaze landed on Carlotta's left hand. She eyed the sparkling engagement ring with a low whistle. "Well, well, did Detective Terry finally come to his senses?"

"Nope," came the sound of Jack's voice.

Carlotta looked to the right to see the big man standing outside the door leading back to the desks and offices. A black scowl hung over his craggy face.

Carlotta exchanged a rueful glance with Brook, then she conjured up a cheerful smile. "Hi, Jack. Thanks for making time for me."

"Now I have *five* minutes, and I was just leaving. You'll have to walk with me."

"Okay," she agreed, determined not to be put off by his brusqueness. The man was capable of swinging from teasing sarcasm to vexation in the space of a few sentences.

She waved goodbye to Brook then followed him back to the hallway where she fell in step beside him. With a little blip of pleasure she noted he was wearing clothes she'd helped him shop for, and carrying the briefcase she'd convinced him to buy now that his job liaising with the GBI required him to attend more meetings.

"Are you on your way to a call?" she asked.

"Nope," he said in a clipped tone. "Just trying to get home at a decent time for once."

Not for the first time, she wondered where 'home' was for Jack—he'd withheld so many details about his life from her. For all she knew, he could live in a mansion, or an extended-stay hotel.

But considering how quickly he'd arrived to help her when she'd discovered Walt Tully hiding in a boat at a Lake Lanier marina, she reasoned he must live somewhere near the large body of water.

"If this is about the wedding," he said as they entered the stairwell, "being Best Man wasn't my idea."

With effort, she maintained her smile. "Coop told me."

He grunted, looking straight ahead. "And you're okay with it?"

She injected a light tone into her voice as they reached the ground floor. "Why wouldn't I be?"

Jack gave a curt nod, as if that was that. "Then what's on your mind?" He held open the door to the parking area, then followed her into the hot stickiness of the day.

"I, um, learned something I think you should know."

"About?"

She wet her lips. "About Patricia Alexander's death."

He stopped so abruptly, she walked past him. When she turned back, his face was stony. "Not this again."

Irritation barbed through her chest. "Yes, this again. It could be important, Jack."

He pinched the bridge of his nose, then started walking again, faster. "*Three* minutes."

"Okay," she said, jogging to keep up with him. "But first... I have a confession to make."

He didn't break stride. "Go on."

She swallowed. "After Patricia's body was removed from the hotel room, I kind of... went back into the room and took photos."

He closed his eyes briefly. "By 'went' in, I assume you mean 'broke' in?"

"I had the key code to her door." She took a deep breath. "Also, I... found something the police overlooked."

Another slow blink. "What was it?"

"A used condom."

He gave a little shrug. "So she had sex before she died."

"Or maybe it wasn't hers," she said, launching into her theory of the switched makeup cases all while trotting to keep up with him. As they reached the dark sedan he drove, she was winding down.

"So," she said, stopping to catch her breath, "if my suspicions are right, the used condom in my freezer could belong to Senator Max Reeder, and Colleen Mason's death might not have been a suicide."

Jack's face was turning dark red. "You have the condom... in your freezer?"

"Yes. And I already had the contents analyzed for DNA—the profile came back of Russian descent, so it couldn't belong to Trevor Biondi, because he's African American, and it couldn't belong to Patricia's blind date John Smythe, because he's Asian."

Jack's face purpled. "You had the contents *analyzed*?" He scoffed. "You've really got Coop wrapped around your... finger."

She scowled. "Coop doesn't know anything about this. I did it myself."

"How?" He held up his hand. "Don't answer that." Then he squinted. "Wait—how do you know John Smythe is Asian?"

"I, uh, came into the possession of Patricia's phone and texted him."

"You have her phone?"

"And all her personal effects from the hotel room. I could re-create the scene from the photos I took."

Jack lifted his key fob to unlock the doors of his car with a *chirp-chirp.*

"What do you think?" she prodded.

"I think," he said carefully, "that your time is up." He opened the door of the sedan.

"You don't believe me?"

His mouth tightened. "I believe you should be too busy trying on wedding gowns to be concocting epic murder scenarios from a series of unrelated events."

She frowned. "For your information, I've tried on dozens of gowns—maybe hundreds. And yet I've still found time to think about the murder of a friend."

"Except. Patricia. Alexander. Wasn't. Murdered," he said through gritted teeth.

Carlotta's chin went up. "But what if she was? What if the senator somehow pulled off not one, but *two* murders while the entire world was watching?" She angled her head. "Including you, Jack."

When he didn't respond, she sighed. "Just tell me you'll think about it."

Instead of answering, he swung into his vehicle and slammed the door—hard.

She gave him a lethal look, then turned to go. His car engine started, then the sound of the window zooming down reached her.

"Carlotta."

She turned back to find him studying her.

"Why are you trying on hundreds of wedding gowns? I thought that hoity-toity designer from the wedding expo said he'd set you up. What was his name? Jett?"

"Jarold Jett," she murmured. The man *had* promised to design a gown for her when she was ready to walk down the aisle... how on earth could she have forgotten? She brightened. "You're right. Thanks, Jack."

Jack zoomed up the window, then put the car in gear and took off.

Carlotta frowned after him, as always, perplexed by his hot and cold behavior. After all they'd been through together, the man remained a mystery.

Then a thought slid into her mind.

Jack was on his way home? This was her chance to follow him and find out where and how the man lived.

Not that it was any of her business anymore.

But it would be amusing—and could come in handy—to have something on the man.

Intrigued, she hurried to her car, unlocked it, and climbed inside. After starting the engine, she steered in the direction Jack had driven.

On the one hand, a white Miata wasn't the best car for tailing someone. On the other hand, Jack didn't know the Miata had been restored and that she was driving it.

She headed toward the part of the interstate known as the Connector because two main corridors ran together for a while. Sure enough, when she was a traffic light back from merging onto the thoroughfare, she spotted his car. When the light turned, she drove assertively to get through it and eased onto the ramp six cars behind him.

Because it was pre-rush hour, the Interstate wasn't yet wall-to-wall with cars. Pushing aside the thought of the nightmare traffic on the return trip, she followed his car at a good distance. When he merged onto I-85 northbound, it strengthened her belief he was headed toward Lake Lanier. Thirty minutes later her suspicions were confirmed when he merged onto I-985 toward the lake.

She took care to hang back on the less traveled roadway, keeping his sedan in sight. At a sign announcing the exit for a handful of marinas—including Redbird Marina where Tracey had been stashing her fugitive father—Jack's turn signal flashed on. Carlotta slowed and followed, allowing several cars to stay between them. As she'd suspected, he apparently lived close to the marina. In one of the sprawling, regal homes scattered along the lakefront? Or an A-frame cabin tucked among the pine trees? The latter seemed more suited to the alpha man who was allegedly fond of fishing.

But to her surprise, his next turn was into a marina adjacent to Redbird. She reasoned he must have a fishing boat moored in one of the slips. She slowed, then drove past the entrance, turned around and circled back. When she pulled into the parking lot that sloped sharply toward the water, she spotted Jack below climbing out of his car, parked close to the water in spots reserved for residents.

She put her car in park and retrieved a pair of binoculars from her bag. From the higher vantage point, she could easily track the big man. He strolled a few yards to a casual walk-up eatery and placed an order. The guy in the window handed Jack a bottle of beer. Jack walked to a nearby picnic table and removed his jacket, then loosened his tie. He leaned against the picnic table, then lifted the beer for a drink. Carlotta marveled at being able to study him when he didn't know he was being watched. When the man wasn't scowling, he was devastatingly handsome.

But he had something on his mind because his body language was fidgety. He kept rubbing his eyes with forefinger and thumb, and grimacing. She wondered wryly if she'd caused any of his discomfort by bringing up Patricia's case, then reasoned Jack had plenty of other cases to worry about. He'd probably already forgotten their conversation.

The man at the window waved to him. Jack pushed away from the picnic table, then walked over to pay the man and took away a sack of food. She watched as he stepped onto the dock of the marina and made his way past several boats of all sizes, then down a side dock. He walked all the way to the end and stopped in front of a boat that stood out from the others. While every other houseboat at the marina was gleaming white fiberglass, this houseboat was wood. Through the binoculars she took in the details. It was at least fifty feet long, the color of aged teak, trimmed in navy. She knew practically nothing about boats and even she could tell it was special. Carlotta shook her head in wonder—of course Jack lived on a boat. It was so... *him.*

And no wonder he'd reached the Redbird marina so quickly when she'd called him in distress—he lived within a stone's throw.

She smiled to herself—the fact that Walt Tully had been hiding out practically under Jack's nose had to have smarted.

Jack boarded the rear of the boat, then settled onto a cushioned bench that flanked the entrance, propped up his booted feet, and tipped up his bottle of beer. He stared out of the water, seemingly in no hurry to eat. The man looked to be at peace, reveling in his solitude. Carlotta was suddenly aware there was no reason to stay any longer, yet she was reluctant to leave. Jack reached for the phone at his belt, then scrolled with his thumb and put the phone to his ear. Three seconds later, her phone rang.

She nearly dropped the binoculars, then glanced at the screen to see who was calling.

Jack Terry.

Did he know she'd followed him? With her pulse pounding in her ears, she connected the call with one hand, keeping the binoculars focused on him. "Hi, Jack."

"Hi, Carlotta." He sighed. "Okay... I'll think about it."

A smile curved her mouth. "Thank you, Jack."

He ended the call. She watched him return the phone to his belt, then pull his hand down his face, as if he already regretted making the call. When he reached for the sack of food, she decided it was time to leave.

But as she lowered the binoculars, something else caught her eye—the name on the back of his boat, spelled out in white cursive letters. *Serena.*

Carlotta pushed her tongue into her cheek. Who the heck was Serena?

CHAPTER 5

"MEG'S DAD hates me," Wes said to Chance. He ran a brush over a dirty golf ball, then dropped it into a plastic bin with a mound of others. The Lindbergh Family Driving Range wouldn't open for another hour, but they still had loads of crummy maintenance to do to get ready.

This place sucked a big hairy one.

Chance snorted, then resumed divvying the cleaned balls into individual buckets. "Dude, that's what dads do—they hate the guy their daughter likes. Look at me—Hannah's dad said I wasn't good enough to date her."

"*Date* her? Did you tell him the horse was already out of the barn?"

"No. Hannah hasn't worked up the courage to tell him we're married, and that we have a kid on the way."

"Jesus."

"I mean I know I'm not book smart like you," Chance said. "And I'm not as good-looking as you. And I'm fat. And I used to sell drugs and pornography. And I was a pimp."

"Uh-huh," Wes said, starting to feel a tad better about himself.

"But at least I've never been arrested like you," Chance said. "Never broke into the courthouse computer system, never got messed up with loan sharks, never got hooked on Oxy, never passed counterfeit money at a casino, and I'm not wearing an ankle bracelet."

"Uh-huh," Wes said, his confidence plummeting again.

"But I love Hannah," Chance said, jabbing his finger in the air. Then he winced and grabbed his arm. "Ow. I think I pulled something."

"I love Meg, too," Wes said miserably. "But Dr. Vincent won't even let me see her."

"But you talk to her, right?"

"Occasionally. They watch her like a hawk, though, so we barely get to have a conversation."

"I guess they're paranoid after she was kidnapped and all. Can't really blame them for that."

Wes stifled a groan of frustration—except her parents had him and Randolph to thank for bringing her home. "I suppose."

Chance sighed. "What are we gonna do to prove ourselves?"

Wes bounced a golf ball into the bin with more force than necessary. "I don't think they're going to give us a chance to prove ourselves."

"I'm serious, Dude. Can you help me get better?"

Wes studied his chubby, slovenly, stoner friend and his earnest expression. "Sure, man. Whatever you need."

Chance lifted his shirt and grabbed two handfuls of belly. "Can you start with this?"

"If you quit smoking weed, you won't have the munchies all the time."

Chance looked pained. "Okay."

"And it wouldn't hurt you to get some exercise."

Chance snapped his fingers, then gestured to the big raking machine that sat outside. "I could walk around to pick up balls instead of running the scooper."

"You'll be skinny in no time," Wes agreed.

Chance grinned. "Thanks, man." Then his face clouded. "What about the rest of me?"

"One step at a time."

At the sound of a car engine, they both craned to see Randolph's big SUV pull up.

"Your dad's early," Chance said, sounding happy.

"Yeah," Wes said, massaging the knot high in his stomach that always formed when he had to interact with his father. He was beyond grateful to him for arranging to rescue Meg, but on nearly every other aspect of life, he and his dad were not on the same page.

Or even in the same book.

A few seconds later, Randolph unlocked the door and stuck his head inside. "Wes, come and take a ride with me."

"Good morning, Mr. Wren," Chance said.

"Morning. Think you can handle the opening alone, Chance?"

"Sure thing, Mr. Wren."

"Great. We'll be back in an hour or so."

Wes wiped his hands on a golf towel, then gave his buddy a nod and followed Randolph back to his SUV. "What's up?"

The black eye he'd given his dad when Randolph had tried to restrain him from going to the airport to fly to Europe had faded to pale green. "I ordered a new sign for the business, thought you and I could pick it up."

"Okay," Wes said, although secretly he dreaded making small talk for the duration of the trip. This new pleasantness between them was more uncomfortable than the simmering anger from before. He climbed into the passenger seat and put on his seatbelt.

"I brought you a coffee and donut," Randolph said, gesturing to the console.

Wes reached for the lidded cup. "Thanks."

Randolph turned the vehicle around and pulled onto the road heading toward the interstate. "Your mom said to come by sometime."

He winced when the bitter coffee hit his tongue. He wanted to add sugar, but he knew his dad would think that was weak. "Between my hours at the driving range and the morgue, I don't have a lot of free time."

Randolph's mouth twitched downward. "Hopefully you can work off your community hours quickly."

"I don't mind working with Coop."

"I like Coop, but I don't understand why he wants to waste his medical degree working with the dead."

"Someone's gotta do it."

His dad grunted. "It doesn't have to be you. How's Meg?"

Wes shifted in his seat. "Okay, I guess. Her dad still doesn't want me coming around, but we talk every day."

"And she's keeping her word?"

Wes took another drink and swallowed. "I sat in on her debriefing with Jack Terry. She told him she didn't know the name of the person who rescued her from the house where she was being held."

"Good."

"But she might have implied he was American."

Randolph made a rueful noise. "Not ideal, but hopefully it'll end there."

Wes hesitated, then voiced his primary concern. "Jack Terry doesn't like to leave loose ends."

Randolph gave a little laugh. "You're telling me. The man forced my hand by reopening my case."

"So why not just tell him Birch rescued Meg? Why the secrecy?"

"Because Birch may or may not have committed other crimes when he rescued Meg."

Wes's eyes bugged. "He killed her captors?"

"I honestly don't know," Randolph said. "No one needs to know."

"I don't understand… if he killed sex traffickers, he should get an award."

"It doesn't work like that. Birch needs to protect his identity."

Wes gave a nervous little laugh. "What is he, some kind of mercenary?"

Randolph's expression hardened. "It's best if we don't talk about it."

"How do you even know him?" Wes pressed.

His dad was quiet for the length of two long draws on his coffee, then he sighed. "Before I met your mother, I did what Birch does."

Wes blinked. "What, exactly?"

Randolph pulled his hand over his mouth. "Worked for the highest bidder."

At his father's cagey tone, his pulse jumped. "Doing what?"

"Whatever needed to be done," Randolph said. "Mostly surveillance and courier work."

Wes wet his lips. "Did you ever kill anyone?"

In the silence that followed, he decided he'd let his imagination run away with him.

"No one who didn't deserve it," Randolph said quietly.

Wonder washed over Wes—he didn't know his father at all… was Randolph Wren a made up name?

"But I gave up that life when I met your mother," his dad continued. "I got into day-trading, and used the money I earned to invest in the firm." Randolph turned his head and gave Wes a pointed look. "This is our secret. Even your mother doesn't know."

His chest billowed from the honor his dad had bestowed upon him—his trust. His lips parted. "Okay."

"Okay," Randolph said with a nod. The subject appeared to be closed.

Wes took another drink of coffee and stared straight ahead, trying to process his father's revelations. He understood a little more about Randolph's standoffish personality… and why he was able to elude the authorities for so long. He was in awe of everything his father had done, and hoped this shared confidence was the beginning of a closer relationship—he already felt closer to the man who had been absent for so much of his life. Happiness bubbled in his chest.

They made small talk about Carlotta's wedding—Coop had asked him to be a groomsman, and Randolph was pleased Carlotta wanted him to walk her down the aisle. Wes took it as a good sign that she'd put the business of Randolph not being her biological father behind her.

"It'll be a happy day," Randolph said.

"Uh-huh," Wes murmured, keeping his concerns to himself. What did he know about relationships? He couldn't even get in the same room with his girlfriend.

"Here we are." Randolph put on his car blinker, then turned into the parking lot of Signs and More.

Wes climbed out and walked with him to the entrance. "Why did you buy a new sign for the driving range?"

Randolph made a thoughtful noise. "Business is booming, and I think we need to move away from the family brand, put our name on it. I made an offer for the adjacent piece of land and it was accepted yesterday." He grinned. "We break ground on a nine-hole golf course in the fall."

Wes's stomach pinched—he hated the golf business. "Wow."

"At first I was disappointed that your poker playing didn't work out," Randolph said, breezing over the fact that Wes had been caught cheating at a private tournament, beat within an inch of his life, and blacklisted from local competitions. "But then I realized maybe it's for the best." He opened the door and waved Wes inside.

Wes walked across the threshold and scanned the interior of the warehouse-size room behind the front counter. Colorful signs of every size, from handheld to billboards, lined the walls. Everyone needed signs, it seemed—churches, Realtors, restaurants. Political signs for Senator Max Reeder dominated one corner. Then Wes's gaze fell on a newly minted green and yellow sign against a far wall.

Wren & Son Golf Center.

He thought he might be sick.

CHAPTER 6

"A WEDDING?" Dr. Denton said, unable to hide his surprise.

Carlotta leaned forward to show her engagement ring to her psychologist. "Coop proposed two weeks ago."

"Congratulations," the man said, sitting back in his chair. "Are you happy about it?"

Carlotta frowned, then laughed. "Of course I am—I said yes, didn't I?"

He nodded. "I'm just saying it seems rather sudden."

"Not at all—I've known Coop for a long time."

"I mean rather sudden after the death of your former fiancé."

She squirmed in the upholstered chair opposite the older man she'd been seeing for a few months. "It might seem that way, but I'd let go of the idea of a future with Peter a while before he was killed."

"I see." He made a few notes in a notebook. "The last time you were here, you said you believed the fugitive Walter Tully was responsible for Mr. Ashford's death?"

"That's right. Walt Tully has since been apprehended."

"Yes, I saw it on the news."

"In fact, I found him," Carlotta said. "Walt tried to kill me too, by tossing me off a dock."

The doctor's eyes widened. "You found a fugitive the GBI couldn't locate?"

"That's right." She wet her lips. "And I found out something else about Walt Tully."

"Do you want to share?"

"He's... my biological father."

Dr. Denton squinted. "Why do you believe that?"

"DNA doesn't lie."

"You had a DNA test?"

"Yes."

He made more notes. "So Mr. Tully knows?"

"No. Only you... and my mother, of course, but she doesn't know I know." She pressed her lips together. "I haven't even told Coop yet."

"That's understandable. You'll probably need some time to process the news yourself."

"But Walt's not my father," she said. "Just a sperm donor. Randolph is my father... I've asked him to walk me down the aisle."

"That's nice. A wedding should be a family affair. So you've set a date?"

"In a little over five weeks."

"That's soon."

"I want to get it behind me." As soon as the words left her mouth, she wanted them back.

"That's a curious way to describe a life event as important as a wedding."

She smiled. "I just mean that I love Coop and I don't want to wait."

"And what's the harm in waiting?"

"Anything could happen," she said with a shrug. "Especially the way my life's been going. I'd like some stability."

"And you think Coop will provide that stability."

"Yes." She studied her nails. "Coop is... easy. Easy to love, I mean."

He nodded. "But emotions can run high during a wedding. It's not unusual for couples to argue."

She shook her head. "Coop and I don't argue... he's... easy."

"Yes, you said that already. So plans for the wedding are going well?"

"I haven't found a dress yet... or filled out the gift registry... or planned the honeymoon."

"Is there a reason you're putting off those decisions?"

She pushed to her feet and turned to study his book shelf. "I've been preoccupied with the unsolved murder of my friend."

"Your former fiancé?"

She turned back toward him. "No, my coworker, Patricia."

He glanced at his notebook. "Oh, yes... the last time you were here you said you were convinced her death wasn't an accident."

"That's right. And I'm even more convinced now." She sighed. "I feel guilty planning a wedding when Peter and Patricia's deaths are both unresolved."

The man coughed lightly. "Carlotta... Peter was killed in jail by another inmate."

"But probably orchestrated by someone on the outside."

"And your friend's death was ruled accidental."

She gave a dismissive wave. "I told you before, that's because the police didn't have all the facts. But they do now. I told Jack everything."

"Jack?"

"Detective Jack Terry."

"Yes, you've mentioned him. He knows Randolph isn't your biological father."

"That's right."

"But the man you're going to marry doesn't know?"

Irritation blipped in her chest. "I just haven't gotten around to telling Coop. It won't change how he feels about me."

"I don't doubt that," the doctor said. "But it might change how you feel about him... it might bring you closer."

"We're already close," she said, exasperated. "We're getting *married*."

He smiled. "The wedding you can't seem to find time to plan."

"Now that Walt Tully is in custody, and Jack is going to look into Patricia's death, my mind is clear," she said lightly, setting aside the facts that Walt had denied putting a hit on Peter, and Jack hadn't yet contacted her for details on the information she'd uncovered.

"Good," Dr. Denton said with a nod. "Maybe you can set aside these mysteries you seem to involve yourself in, and get on with your own life."

Carlotta manufactured a smile. "That's the plan."

CHAPTER 7

"BANANA PANCAKES or chocolate chip?" Coop asked from the stove.

"Both!" Prissy shouted.

"Both," Valerie seconded.

"Both," Carlotta agreed.

He grinned and carried a pan to the table, doled out one round of pancakes then returned with a second pan to top them off with another flavor.

"Thank you!"

"Thank you, Coop."

"Thanks… you." Carlotta smiled at him, thinking she was going to have to come up with a better endearment for her husband-to-be. Darling? Honey? Sweetheart? The man seemed so at ease in the kitchen of the townhome she shared with Wes. Her mind traveled back to when she'd first met him… she'd been sitting at this very table when Wes had introduced his boss for his new job of moving bodies for the morgue.

So much had happened since then.

Prissy smeared her cakes with peanut butter, then doused the stack with warm syrup. Valerie did the same. And Carlotta did the same.

Coop took a seat at the table and laughed at their identical plates. "You three are pretty peas in a pod—you look alike, you sound alike, and you like the same things. Randolph is a lucky man."

Valerie slid a questioning look to Carlotta as she put her napkin on her lap. Carlotta suspected her mother was wondering if Coop knew Randolph wasn't her biological father. She still hadn't told him, and frankly, didn't see the need. It wouldn't change anything, she rationalized, turning back to her breakfast.

"Coop, where did you learn to cook?" Valerie asked.

He shrugged. "I worked in restaurants to put myself through med school, picked up a few tricks. And I've lived on my own for all of my adult life, so it was either fast food or learn to feed myself."

"You'll have to cook after you and Carlotta get married," Prissy said through a mouth full of food. "Wes says she's hopeless."

They all laughed, but Carlotta just shrugged. "Cooking isn't my strong suit."

"It was never mine, either," Valerie admitted.

"I can't cook either," Prissy declared, then turned an earnest expression toward Coop. "We're good at shopping for clothes, though."

He laughed heartily. "I noticed. Valerie, Carlotta says your hanger is really taking off."

"It's called the StyleMe Hanger," Prissy said.

"Carlotta invented it," Valerie said. "I'm just marketing it."

"Which I wouldn't have thought of," Carlotta remarked. "Mom already has prototypes made and will be taking orders at trade shows this summer."

"And she has a meeting with one of the home shopping networks," Prissy added.

"Two successful businesswomen in the family," Coop said.

Valerie reached over to squeeze his hand. "Only because you fixed me, Coop."

Behind his glasses, he blushed adorably. "Your neurologist gets all the credit—I only voiced my suspicions about your condition."

Carlotta's chest warmed at how good Coop was with her family—she was indebted to him for giving her mother a healthy future.

"I knew you and Carlotta would be married someday," Valerie said. "I saw the writing on the wall in Vegas."

"Really?" Coop asked. "That long ago you suspected we'd end up together?"

Valerie smiled. "I mean, Carlotta showed me a picture where she'd written your name on a wall."

Coop shot a quizzical look toward Carlotta. "Hm?

Her face warmed. "There was an old coffee shop in Vegas... in the bathroom the walls were covered with names and little messages." She patted her mouth with her napkin, suddenly embarrassed. "I guess I was feeling a little dreamy... I got it in my mind that I would write the name of the person I hoped to spend my life with."

An expression of wonder fell over his face. "And that was me?"

She nodded. "That was you."

He reached for her hand, then brought it to his mouth for a kiss. From the way his eyes shined she realized with a start that Coop had never felt as if he was her first choice. Guilt stabbed at her, and she vowed to make it up to him.

"That's when I saw Mom's name on the wall," she continued. "Mom had written it there when she and Dad arrived in Vegas. It's how I knew she was close by." She reached for her phone. "I think I saved the picture." She sorted her stored photos by date and found it, then turned the screen for them to see. "There's where I wrote Coop's name... and there's Mom's name just below."

"Wow," Prissy said.

"It was meant for you to find us," Valerie said.

Carlotta nodded, marveling that the clues to her parents' whereabouts had revealed themselves when she was at her lowest points.

"And the two of you were meant to be," Valerie added, casting a warm smile over the couple.

The doorbell rang, then the door opened and Hannah clomped in. "Hi, all. I smelled pancakes from the driveway."

"There's plenty," Coop said. "Help yourself."

"I will," Hannah said, picking up a plate and piling it high. "This baby is hungry all the time."

"Carlotta," Prissy said, "are you and Coop going to have babies?"

Carlotta blinked, then exchanged an amused glance with Coop. "Um..."

"We haven't talked about it," Coop supplied casually.

"My friend Mary Beth Thompson says you have to do more than talk."

Hannah howled laughing, and Coop hid a smile behind his napkin.

"You and I will discuss it later," Valerie said to Prissy, then turned to Carlotta. "When are we going shopping again for your wedding dress?"

Carlotta cut into her pancakes. "I might not have to. A while back I worked at a wedding expo, and I got to meet Jarold Jett."

"The designer?" Prissy asked, her eyes wide.

Carlotta wasn't surprised her little sister knew of him. "That's right. I did him a favor—"

"She saved his ass," Hannah interjected.

"—and Jarold told me if I ever needed a wedding gown to let him know. I'd forgotten all about it until—" She caught herself. "Until a friend reminded me. I sent Jarold a DM and he responded right away that he'd send me a dress."

"What if you don't like it?" Hannah asked.

The same thought had crossed her mind.

"I'm sure it'll be beautiful," Valerie soothed.

"You'll make any dress look beautiful," Coop added.

She smiled her appreciation—the man made her feel adored.

"If you don't like the wedding dress he sends, maybe I'll wear it when I marry Jack," Prissy announced.

A few seconds of awkward silence fell over the table, until Coop broke it with a laugh. "You're going to marry Jack?"

Prissy nodded. "When I grow up."

"He'd be lucky to have you," Coop said, then cleared his throat. "Jack's going to be the Best Man in our wedding."

"He is?" Prissy, Valerie, and Hannah said in unison. Prissy looked excited, Valerie and Hannah less so.

"Yes," Coop said, suddenly sounding uncertain.

"Yes," Carlotta seconded, giving him a reinforcing smile. "Coop and Jack have been friends for a long time."

Carlotta's phone buzzed. She glanced at the screen to see Lindy Russell's name. "My former boss is calling, I should get this."

She stepped away from the table and connected the call. "Hi, Lindy."

"Hi, Carlotta. An opportunity came across my desk I think you'll be perfect for if you have time. Delinda Reeder is looking for a personal shopper."

Carlotta's heart rate sped up. "Senator Reeder's wife?"

"Yes. She's looking for someone to help her choose a wardrobe for the events she'll attend while campaigning with her husband. It could mean great exposure, Carlotta, and a handsome commission. Are you interested?"

Interested in the chance to gain access to the man she suspected had something to do with Patricia's death?

"Absolutely."

CHAPTER 8

"CARLOTTA WREN for Mrs. Reeder."

The black security speaker emitted static, then a male voice sounded. "Please pull through the gate and follow the driveway around to the garage."

The ornate metal gate in front of her car swung open onto a pristine stone driveway that led to a sprawling gray mansion of indeterminate age. Fighting a bout of butterflies, Carlotta followed the curving driveway to the main entrance of the stately home. A suited man with a nameplate that read "Doug" directed her to park in front of the six-car garage. Noting the gadgets at his belt, she assumed he was a security guard. No doubt the Reeders employed a staff of helpers and protectors.

She gave her makeup and hair one last glance in the rear view mirror, then alighted from the convertible. Even the sticky humidity seemed milder here in the shade of tall hardwoods and manicured flowering trees.

The man led her to the front door, where he handed her off to a naturally pretty blond woman who looked to be about thirty. After an approving glance over Carlotta's green Chanel pantsuit and black Gucci sandals, the woman extended her hand.

"Hello, Ms. Wren. I'm Emma Wallace, Delinda's assistant."

Carlotta shook her hand. "It's nice to meet you." She reached into her bag and withdrew a business card. "Here's my complete contact information."

The woman took the card, then tucked it into a portfolio she carried. "Please come in."

Carlotta followed her inside to an expansive entryway that splintered off into hallways and wings. The décor was luxurious, but understated, the perfect tone for a politician's home.

Her senses were on high alert to discern what she could about Delinda Reeder's style aesthetic. She wanted this job for a laundry list of reasons, so she needed to bring her A-game. She was more than qualified to dress the woman, but much of a personal shopper's success depended on the chemistry between them and their client.

And she was worried the senator's wife would remember her from Peter's funeral. The Reeders were friends with the Ashfords, had attended the funeral and witnessed Peter's mother accuse Carlotta of abandoning Peter.

"Mrs. Reeder is on a conference call," Emma said. She asked me to escort you to her dressing room, where refreshments are waiting. Right this way."

Carlotta followed the woman down a hallway, then up a sweeping set of stairs to the second floor. Quality art pieces adorned the walls, but family photos dominated. Furnishings were lush, but mismatched. The house had a comfortable, lived-in feel.

"What a beautiful home," Carlotta said.

"The house has been in Delinda's family for generations."

Carlotta had researched Delinda Reeder, who seemed destined for an amazing life from birth. She'd been born into old money, attended the best private schools before completing her medical degree at Emory. She was a Board-certified cosmetic surgeon and by all reports, had built a successful practice on her own before marrying Max Reeder, hotshot defense attorney with political ambitions. They made for a beautiful media couple, both slim and attractive, with five smiling kids, two of whom had been adopted. Some reports named Delinda as the engine behind her husband's success, but in interviews Carlotta had studied, the woman gave all the credit to her hard-working and compassionate husband.

"Is the Senator home by chance?"

Suspicion flickered in Emma's eyes. "No. The Senator is at his office."

"I'm a supporter," Carlotta improvised. "I was hoping to meet him."

"Maybe some other time." Emma stopped at a decorative table in the hall where a single sheet of paper lay next to a pen. "I hope you don't mind—everyone the Reeders employ must sign a non-disclosure agreement."

Carlotta guessed she shouldn't be surprised—the Reeders were high profile and had to protect themselves from...

People like her.

"Of course," she said, then skimmed the agreement. She was agreeing not to disclose any personal or professional information about the Reeder family she might directly or indirectly learn in the pursuit of duties she was hired to undertake. But Carlotta also knew that signing an NDA didn't commit a person to silence if they had knowledge of a crime. The documents were designed primarily to scare people, secondarily to recoup damages if someone blabbed juicy details to the press. She signed her name and dated the form.

"Thank you," Emma said primly, then walked across the hall to a closed door. "This is Mrs. Reeder's dressing room," she said before turning the knob.

Carlotta stepped in and glanced around, surmising a bedroom suite had been converted to the large closet. A custom storage system of pale wood lined the perimeter of the room—cabinets, drawers and shelves, floor to ceiling. Framed photographs made up most of the room's decoration, along with a few well-placed plants. The tri-paneled mirror and warm, pink-hued lighting rivaled a boutique setting. In the center two white loveseats with curved legs faced each other over a table laden with a tea service, finger sandwiches, and fresh fruit.

"Very nice," Carlotta offered.

Emma smiled. "Mrs. Reeder thought you might want to assess her current wardrobe before suggesting additions that would be appropriate for the many events she has scheduled in the next few months."

"I was going to suggest the same thing," Carlotta said with a nod.

"Can I pour you some tea?"

"I'm fine, thank you." She gestured to the closed closet doors. "Shall I wait for Mrs. Reeder, or is it all right if I get started?"

Emma glanced at her watch. "It could be a few more minutes so you can get started if you like. How can I help?"

"Do you have a list of the types of events she'll be attending?"

"I'll print a calendar, give me a few minutes."

The woman hesitated, then left the room. Carlotta immediately lasered in on the photographs in the room. They were family photos, mostly of Delinda with her children who looked to range in age from a son in his late twenties to a little girl of five or so. Strangely, there were no photos of the Senator, although admittedly, it seemed more of a room celebrating motherhood. Homemade "I Love You, Mom" cards and various trinkets bearing the word "Mother" written in the uneven hand of a child said the woman was beloved by her kids.

Mindful the assistant could return at any time, Carlotta began to open the cabinet doors and drawers to reveal racks and stacks of clothing grouped by type—blouses here, skirts there, jackets over there—and loads of shoes and accessories. The fact that the woman was organized, though, would make her job easier. Most items were of the best quality, but some were dated, or simply uninspiring. Many of the garments she recognized from the digital look-book she'd put together of photos she'd found of Delinda Reeder. The most interesting garments she pulled out to hang on a rack, then took photographs on her tablet.

Emma returned to the room. "Here's a calendar of the events Delinda will be attending over the next few months."

Carlotta took the stapled pages offered and scanned them—community forums, parades, school events, fundraisers, dinners, lunches, breakfasts, brunches. "She's a very busy woman."

"Yes," Emma said. "And when Senator Reeder gets the party nomination, she'll be even more busy."

"*If* Senator Reeder gets the party nomination," came a voice from the hallway.

Delinda Reeder appeared at the door wearing a yellow shirtdress and a winning smile. She looked vibrant and a decade younger than her fifty-five years. "You must be the woman who's going to make me look good." She extended her hand to Carlotta. "I'm Delinda."

Carlotta smiled and clasped her hand. "I'm Carlotta Wren. And if I may say so, you already look good, Mrs. Reeder. That's a Veronica Beard dress, if I'm not mistaken. Beautiful."

"You're not mistaken," the woman said, then turned to her assistant. "Emma, I believe we're in good hands. And please, Carlotta, call me Delinda."

Carlotta inclined her head. "Thank you for this opportunity. I took the liberty of skimming your wardrobe, I hope that was okay."

"Absolutely, I appreciate your enthusiasm. As you can see, I haven't been shopping in a very long time."

"But you have some great pieces to build on. Can you show me some of your favorite outfits?"

"I prefer pants, but I've found dresses to be the most versatile when I have back to back events." She walked to a cabinet and pulled out a half dozen dresses. "These are some of my go-tos."

"Yes, very nice... but maybe too frequently photographed at this point?" Carlotta turned her tablet around and swiped through photos of Delinda she'd downloaded, showing her in the same few outfits over and over.

Delinda puffed out her cheeks in an exhale. "So I see. This is why I'm garnering so many snarky comments on social media. It shouldn't matter what the candidate's wife looks like, but it does."

"I was just thinking how youthful you look," Carlotta offered.

Delinda made a rueful noise. "I've been able to stave off time with good skincare and fillers, but apparently my wardrobe needs a full facelift. I'm going to be straight with you, Carlotta. I need to appeal to women voters. I have to look put-together, but not *too* good, if that makes sense."

"She needs to look relatable," Emma added.

"And my clothes have to travel well, and be comfortable." Delinda gave a little laugh. "I know it's a tall order."

"I understand," Carlotta said.

"I have a semi-formal fundraiser coming up in two days' time—is it possible for you to find something for me to wear on such short notice?"

"Yes, of course. I'll put together three looks and have them delivered tomorrow."

"Wonderful." She glanced at her watch. "I'm afraid I have another conference call. Do you need to take my measurements?"

"If you can point out clothes that fit the way you like, I'll go off those measurements."

Delinda grinned. "Excellent." She went from cabinet to cabinet and chose a handful of garments, indicating what she liked about the fit, the length, the fabric. Carlotta took copious notes. "You can take these with you, if you like."

"That will help, yes."

Delinda instructed Emma to bag the clothes for Carlotta. When her assistant left the room, Delinda studied Carlotta, then angled her head. "Have we met before? You look so familiar to me."

Carlotta's pulse spiked. "No, we haven't met before." Not a lie.

The woman gave a dismissive wave. "Forgive me, I see a lot of faces. Do you work for yourself, Carlotta?"

"Yes. In fact, I just launched my own business."

Emma reappeared with the bagged clothing.

"We could use more women entrepreneurs at our events," Delinda said. "I have extra tickets to the fundraiser I mentioned. Will you come and bring a friend?"

It could be her chance to meet the Senator, see the type of people who surrounded him. "Of course."

"Terrific—Emma will take care of you. It's been a pleasure, Carlotta."

"The pleasure's mine."

The woman left the room and walked in the opposite direction. Emma led the way back to the front entrance. "Delinda likes you." Her voice sounded almost... suspicious.

"I like her, too," Carlotta said. "You must enjoy working for her."

"Yes." Emma handed over the bagged clothes, then removed two tickets from her portfolio. "For the fundraiser."

"Thank you," Carlotta said, then glanced at the tickets. "The event is at the Bedford Manor Country Club?"

"You know of it?"

"I do," Carlotta said, pinging with bittersweet memories. "I appreciate your help today."

"It's my job to look out for Delinda." The woman gave her a flat smile, then stepped back and closed the door.

Carlotta pursed her mouth. But on the short walk to her car, Carlotta decided it was natural for the woman to be suspicious and to guard her relationship with the senator's wife. Even so, things had gone better than she'd expected.

'Doug' was nowhere in sight, but as she stopped at the rear of her convertible to stow the bag of clothes, a luxury blue sports car drove up and pulled in next to her. The door opened and out stepped Max Reeder, tall and lean and more handsome in person than he appeared on TV.

"Let me give you a hand."

She was so surprised, she didn't have time to object as he took the bag and flashed her a big smile. "I'm Max."

"Yes, I know," she stammered, irritated with herself for allowing him to affect her. "I'm Carlotta... your wife's personal shopper." She fumbled, then managed to open the small trunk.

"Good," he said, settling the bag inside and sliding his gaze over the length of her. "That means I'll see more of you."

Except the way he said "more of you" did not come across as "more often."

He walked the few steps back to his car that was still running. "Bye, Carlotta." He swung inside and closed the door, then drove up to the garage door that rose as he approached.

Carlotta swallowed hard and walked to the driver's side of her car. She glanced up at the house and saw someone looking out the window. But before she could see a face, they'd disappeared. Feeling unnerved, she hurried into her car and backtracked her way to the metal gate that opened as she drove up to it.

As the gate closed behind her, she couldn't help but feel the ornate hunk of iron was keeping a family's secrets inside.

CHAPTER 9

WES STARED up at the dim light shining in the second floor window and gauged the distance between the farthest reaching limb of the oak tree and the sloped roof.

He could make it.

Probably.

Meg walked past the window again, her slim silhouette outlined in aching detail. He looked away before the blood could rush out of his brain, scouring the chunk of suburban solitude. Luckily for him, the neighborhood shut down at nine o'clock. Meg's parents had probably been asleep for hours. He lay his bicycle in a patch of deep grass, then walked to the tree to see if he could reach the lowest branch. If he made it to the top, he'd call Meg to let him in. If he fell and broke his neck, someone would find him in the morning.

There was one upside to dying painfully from a fall—he wouldn't have to spend the rest of his life at the golf center.

On the second jump, he got one hand around the branch, then pulled himself up. Inside the tree, though, it was pitch black. He pulled out his phone and switched on the flashlight app. There were enough branches overhead to give him hope. He wedged the phone in his mouth and clamped down with his teeth to shine the flashlight above him. Slowly he moved hand over hand to pull himself up and find a foothold that would allow him to reach the next branch and test it gingerly before heaving himself up again.

Halfway up he had to stop to rest. Sweat dripped down his back and sucked his T-shirt to his skin. Gravity pulled at him, and he was afraid if he looked down, he'd give into the urge to fall. Heights had never been his thing, but at this point, it was easier to keep climbing up than to climb down. He took a deep breath, clamped down on the phone again, and pulled himself to a higher branch. At least the limbs were closer together... but they weren't as strong. When he was within reach of the branch that would take him nearest to Meg's window, he ran the flashlight along its length to check its sturdiness.

And dropped his phone.

It hit every branch on the way down, proof that he would do the same if he made a wrong move. He cursed—now he couldn't call her to tell her he was in the tree outside.

Which, he now realized, sounded batshit crazy.

He reached overhead until he felt the thickest branch, then gingerly lifted himself. The branch swayed under his weight... but it held. He was now eye-level with Meg's window, could see her little TV in the corner and the edge of her bed. He used one hand to hang on and one to run along the branch, looking for a twig he could break off to throw.

Instead, he found a clump of small, hard acorns.

Thank you, Jesus.

He separated them and put them in his jeans pocket, then hung on with one hand and heaved an acorn at her window. It fell way short and dropped like a rock.

He sucked at golf, and he'd never make it as a pitcher.

He dug to retrieve another acorn from his pocket and tried again. This one almost made it to the window, then fell. When he threw the third one, he nearly flung himself out of the tree, but at least it struck the glass.

Meg appeared at the window and frowned down at the yard.

"Meg!" he called.

She obviously couldn't hear him, although it sounded as if he was screaming.

He hurried to retrieve another acorn, but dropped it. Meg turned away from the window. He found one last nut in the corner of his pocket, pulled it out and hurled it at the glass. It pinged off, getting her attention again. She opened the window and peered down.

"Meg!"

She startled and pulled back from the window.

"It's me—Wes!"

She squinted into the dark. "Wes? Where the hell are you?"

"I'm... in the tree. I can see you."

She gaped. "You climbed the tree?"

"I wanted to see you."

"You're insane."

"Are you going to let me in?"

She smiled in his direction, shaking her head. "Please don't fall."

Fueled by a new burst of energy, he hugged the horizontal branch and inched his way toward her. When the branch began to sway, he stopped. "I'm going to drop down to the roof."

"It's pretty steep," she said, glancing at the pitch outside her window. "Be careful."

He counted to three, then dropped his legs and swung them as he let go. He hit the roof and skidded a few stomach-clutching inches, then stopped.

"You're giving me a heart attack," Meg said, extending her hand.

He reached up to clasp her hand. When he saw she was wearing the rose gold bracelet he'd given her, adrenaline drove him forward. She pulled and he climbed and finally he tumbled over the window sill into her room. They fell into each other, laughing and kissing while trying to catch their breath.

"I can't believe you did that!"

"Do you think we woke your parents?"

"No. Their room is on the other side of the house. I'm sorry my dad has been such a bear... I'm being patient because I know this situation scared him to death."

"He doesn't seem to mind if Mark visits," Wes groused.

"He knows Mark... and he trusts him. But he'll come around eventually."

Wes had his doubts. "Why were you still awake?"

She pulled back and her face grew pensive. "I haven't been sleeping well since... everything."

He reached forward to stroke her dark blond hair away from her face. "I'm sorry. What can I do?"

"Stay with me," she said, pulling him toward her bed.

She was wearing a pair of silky pj pants and a paper-thin tank top that hugged her slight curves. His body started firing, but he ground his teeth. "I didn't come here for that." Not that he'd turn her down.

"I know," she said. "I'm not ready for that either. But will you stay with me until I go to sleep?"

Wes nodded and followed her to the white four-poster bed with princess canopy. It wasn't at all what he'd pictured for her room, and hinted she might be more vulnerable than her kick-ass personality had led him to believe. He kicked off his tennis shoes and crawled on top of the covers with her, spooning her willowy body to his. He inhaled the floral scent of her hair into his lungs and felt calm bleed through his limbs. He never wanted to let go.

Exhaustion pulled at him… He would close his eyes only for a few minutes…

A faint beeping noise started him awake. The battery on his ankle monitor was running low. He blinked to clear the fog in his mind, then recognized the canopy of Meg's bed and remembered where he was. When he shifted, his muscles felt stiff, no doubt from climbing the tree.

Next to him, Meg was sleeping soundly. Pre-dawn light filtered into her room. He silently gave thanks to the wimpy battery, else he might've slept until daylight, and that would've severely compromised his chances of shimmying back down the tree without being noticed.

He left her bed quietly so he wouldn't disturb her, found and laced up his tennis shoes, then slowly eased up her window. The roof pitch looked steeper in the early light, but he was able to slide down on his back and use his tennis shoes as brakes. When he got close to the tree branch he'd used as a bridge last night, he stood and was able to pull it down to get a handhold. From there he descended branch by branch until he was close enough to the ground to drop. When he landed in the soft dewy grass, he was pleased with himself. Getting down was definitely easier than climbing up had been.

"Good morning."

Wes startled, then turned his head to see Dr. Harold Vincent sitting in a lawn chair next to the tree, holding a coffee mug... and Wes's phone. Since his bike was leaning against the tree trunk, he presumed the man had found it.

Busted.

He considered making a run for it, then realized the jig was up. And the man didn't appear to be armed. "Uh... good morning... sir."

Her father's face was a calm mask of fury. "I thought I made it clear that you were to stay away from Meg."

Wes's mouth tightened. "Meg is old enough to decide who she wants to see."

"Meg has been traumatized. She's not in the right frame of mind to be making decisions. It's my job to protect her from the likes of you."

Wes swallowed hard. "I care about Meg."

"You're out of your league, son. You and your family have a bad reputation, and I don't want it to stain my daughter."

Wes's mouth watered to tell him that he and his family were responsible for Meg's safe return, but his promise to Randolph meant he had to stay silent. He could, at least, defend his future. "I'm going to be a doctor," he blurted.

The man belly-laughed. "Boy, you probably couldn't even pass the college entrance exam."

A retort burned Wes's tongue, but he had the same doubts. He opened his mouth to speak up for himself, but was interrupted by the beep of his ankle monitor. He glanced down to the thick black band to see a red light flashing.

Dr. Vincent arched an eyebrow. "You were saying?"

Wes blinked back hot tears. He had nothing.

The man pushed to his feet and held out Wes's phone. "Here. Leave. If you truly care about Meg, you'll stay away from her."

Wes bit down hard on his tongue to regain his composure, then walked over to take his phone. A jagged crack split the screen. With Harold Vincent's hostile gaze burning into his back, he retrieved his bike, then jumped on and pedaled away, feeling like a loser.

CHAPTER 10

"THANK YOU, have a wonderful evening," the perky hostess said to Carlotta and Hannah, waving toward the entrance of the Bedford Manor Country Club. Beautifully dressed people streamed in ahead of them.

"It's not as fun when we have legit tickets," Hannah complained.

"No, it's much more fun to stand in line wondering if we're going to be booted for counterfeit tickets," Carlotta said wryly.

"Or arrested," Hannah added. "You loved party crashing. And you have to admit, we were good at it."

"We were," Carlotta agreed.

"Have you heard from Jolie lately?"

Jolie was a former coworker at Neiman's she and Hannah had initiated into party crashing, with disastrous results. Still, things had ended well for Jolie.

"I sent her a wedding invitation. I'd love to see her."

"I'd love to see her yummy husband," Hannah said. Then she sighed. "You're going to have a yummy husband, too."

"Your husband is..." Carlotta stopped, unable to lie. "Um, how is that going, by the way?"

"Still working on it," Hannah chirped.

They walked through the entrance of the staid building into the richly furnished lobby, and Carlotta was flooded with memories. Her parents had belonged to the club when she was young and she was considered a debutante, although all of that ended when her parents had skipped town. She'd attended events with Peter when they'd started dating after his wife had died, much to the chagrin of members who'd known her fugitive parents. And she'd been on Randolph's arm during his triumphant return to society after he'd been exonerated.

"I'm surprised you're not having your wedding here," Hannah said.

"They're booked a year in advance," Carlotta said. "Besides, Coop and I much prefer the charm of the Georgian Terrace Hotel."

"No argument from me," Hannah said. "But I would've thought the Georgian would be booked, too."

"They were," Carlotta said. "But they had a cancellation."

"Someone got cold feet?"

"Apparently."

"That happens more than you think," Hannah said. "It's why hotels charge such a hefty deposit. Speaking of the wedding, has your dress arrived?"

"Not yet." She was starting to feel antsy about leaving such a monumental decision in the hands of someone she barely knew.

"What was Coop thinking when he asked Jack to be Best Man?"

Carlotta managed a casual shrug. "I guess he was thinking that he and Jack are old friends."

"How do you feel about it?"

"It's Coop's decision, and Jack seems okay with it."

Hannah's eyebrows climbed. "You talked to Jack?"

"I, uh, told him my theory about the makeup case swap, and it came up."

"Uh-huh. And what did he say about your theory?"

"That he'd think about it."

"Okay, that's something."

"But he hasn't asked me for Patricia's things, or the photos I took."

"In case you haven't noticed, Detective Dickstick isn't the kind of man who can be hurried."

Carlotta frowned. "I noticed."

Hannah turned to scan the crowd. "Explain to me again why we're here."

"We're here," Carlotta said, glancing at faces they passed, "to support my newest client."

Hannah pulled at the side seam of her black Halston cocktail dress. "I take it your newest client doesn't know you suspect her husband of murder?"

"Keep your voice down, and stop fidgeting. You look terrific."

The high neck and long sleeves covered her friend's myriad of tattoos. Her striped hair was slicked back into a chignon that threw her perfect features into relief. When the occasion called for it, Hannah could outshine the most elegant of Buckhead belles.

"I'm getting fat," Hannah groused, pulling at her dress again. "Dammit, I'm going to have to break down and buy some maternity clothes. Will you help me?"

"Of course."

"That's new," Hannah said, nodding at Carlotta's burgundy cold-shoulder sheath dress. "And pretty swank."

"It's by a local designer, Lolly Day. I love her new line, so we struck a deal... I'm representing her brand when I attend events."

"You're getting paid to wear free designer clothes to parties?"

Carlotta grinned. "Don't hate me. Besides, it's not as lucrative as mukbanging."

"And what am I getting out of this? I can't even drink alcohol."

"We won't stay long... I just need to make the rounds. I see more familiar faces than I expected."

Hannah looked past Carlotta's shoulder. "Speaking of."

Carlotta turned to see Tracey Tully Lowenstein heading their way. Her stomach pinched. It was the first time she'd seen the woman since she'd learned they were half-sisters.

"I'm going to the kitchen to see if any of my catering buddies are here," Hannah said, then scooted away.

Tracey glided up with a drink in her hand and a ready smirk. "Carlotta, I haven't seen you since... oh, right, since you had my father arrested and dragged away like a common criminal."

Tracey was already tipsy, Carlotta noticed. She studied the woman's features, looking for shared traits. "I'm sorry things turned out the way they did, Tracey. There's been a lot of heartache all around."

"Not for you," Tracey slurred. "I heard you're marrying that mortician."

Carlotta pressed her lips together. "The Medical Examiner, yes."

She glanced down at Carlotta's engagement ring, then pursed her lips. "Not bad. But just so you know, being married to a doctor isn't all it's cracked up to be."

The woman was unaware that when Carlotta had followed Tracey thinking she was hiding Walt, Carlotta learned Tracey had been following her husband—to his mistress's house. "Is Freddy with you tonight?"

"No," Tracey said, then waved her hand vaguely. "He's into something else tonight."

She didn't doubt that. Compassion for the woman's predicament washed over her. "Tracey, I know we haven't always gotten along, but you and I have a lot in common... and I'd really like for us to be friends."

Tracey recoiled. "What do you and I have in common?"

She chose her words carefully. "I know what it's like to have a father in trouble with the law, and to feel as if people are judging you."

Tracey made a face. "You don't know anything about how I feel. If it weren't for you, my father wouldn't be locked up like an animal."

They were attracting attention from people standing nearby. "Again, I'm so sorry, Tracey," Carlotta murmured. "Enjoy your evening."

She turned and walked toward the bar, then asked for a glass of white wine. While she waited, a woman complimented her dress, and Carlotta told her about the local designer. Sipping from her glass of wine, she moved from one small group to another, chatting with people she knew in passing, and sharing the name of the designer when women commented on her attire.

A murmur moved across the room, and Carlotta looked up to see the senator had arrived, with Delinda on his arm, looking lovely in a blue caped dress, one of the three outfits Carlotta had sent over, and her personal favorite.

"Nicely done."

Carlotta turned to see Delinda's assistant Emma, smartly dressed in a black pantsuit. She inclined her head toward her boss. "Mrs. Reeder has never looked better."

Carlotta smiled. "I'm glad you think so. I'm nearly finished pulling together her new wardrobe—how does Delinda's schedule look this week? We might need an entire day."

"The next few days are light," Emma said. "Let me take a look at the calendar and get back to you."

"Sure," Carlotta said, then glanced back to the other side of the room. "The dark-haired man standing near the Senator—is that their son?"

"Yes, that's Eathan."

From the way the woman's cheeks pinked, Carlotta suspected she had feelings for the man... or perhaps they were involved? "I seem to remember he's an attorney like the Senator?"

"That's right... he's set to follow in his father's footsteps."

Not in every way, Carlotta hoped.

Emma offered a flat smile. "I should go mingle. Have fun."

Carlotta continued to work the room, staying on the perimeter and away from the guests of honor. From a distance she observed the way the couple interacted. Max was deferential to his wife, and often put his hand at her waist, while Delinda seemed to hang on his every word.

They certainly acted like a couple in love.

At that moment, Max Reeder looked up and noticed her. The intensity of his stare sent a finger of unease running between her shoulder blades. Without breaking eye contact, he turned his head and excused himself, then made a beeline for her.

She wanted to run, but took another sip of wine to try to relax as he strode up.

"Carlotta, right?"

She smiled. "You have a good memory, Senator."

"How could I forget such a pretty face?"

She kept smiling.

"I came over to say thank you. My wife has never looked more beautiful."

She inclined her head. "You're welcome. I'm glad you're both pleased with my services."

He molested her with his eyes. "So we'll be seeing more of each other?"

Her skin crawled. "I suppose so."

"Looking forward to it," he said, then turned and greeted someone standing nearby. Unnerved, Carlotta took another drink from her glass and moved away. But when she spotted Tracey, she pivoted and moved in the other direction—directly in the path of Peter's parents. Luckily, they hadn't seen her yet, but Carlotta decided it was time to go. She did not need another public altercation with Mrs. Ashford over her dead son.

She only wished the woman knew she was pushing for answers regarding Peter's death.

Carlotta abandoned her drink at a side table, ducked down a hallway toward the restrooms, and kept walking toward the kitchen. She pushed open the swinging door and peeked inside to see Hannah standing in the middle of the busy kitchen eating a pork chop with her hands.

"Time to go," Carlotta said.

"Okay," Hannah said, taking large bites to finish. She dropped the bone on the tray of a server passing by, then wiped her hands on her dress. "I'm ready." She pointed toward the back of the kitchen. "We can exit here."

"That might be best," Carlotta agreed.

She followed Hannah through the kitchen to a rear service door. When they pushed it open and exited into the dark parking lot next to a smelly dumpster, Hannah grinned "Just like old times."

Carlotta had to laugh. "You're right." And just like that, the craving for a cigarette hit her—hard. Ugh, she'd hoped her unpleasant addiction was behind her. She closed her eyes and willed it to pass.

"While I was in the kitchen," Hannah said in a sing-song voice, "I got some skinny from the catering staff on Max Reeder."

Carlotta's eyes popped open. "What did they say?"

"Apparently he's known to flirt with the help, to the point that some women refuse to work his events."

"Really?" She grunted. "He went out of his way to talk to me tonight. Said he wanted to thank me for making his wife look nice, but he was flirting—and fishing."

"Yeah, but that doesn't mean he's a murderer. Maybe he's just a run of the mill philanderer, who got lucky when his mistress took her own life."

"Maybe," Carlotta agreed.

Max Reeder did seem like the kind of man who had luck on his side.

CHAPTER 11

WES OPENED the door to the tuxedo shop and slid inside. His dad, Coop, and Jack stood in a semi-circle a few feet away. They all turned toward him.

"There he is," Coop said with a smile.

"We've been waiting," Randolph said, his voice tinged with disapproval.

"Sorry," Wes said. "Had to get a new phone."

"What happened to the old one?" his dad asked.

"Dropped it."

"No big deal," Coop said easily. "We've just been catching up. Your dad was telling us about the golf center."

Oh, goody.

They stared at him.

With a start, he realized he'd said that out loud. "Good," he amended. "Business is... really good."

"How's Meg?" Jack asked.

"She's improving."

"Is her memory improving? I'd still like to know more about how she was rescued."

Wes shot a look at Randolph, who pulled on his ear and glanced away.

And dammit, Jack caught it all.

Wes gave a little shrug. "She told you what she knows. She's trying not to dwell on it, you know... moving on."

"Right," Jack said.

"Jack," Coop said, "did you know Wes is helping out at the morgue?"

Jack pursed his mouth. "Working at the golf center for your dad and at the morgue for Coop? You must be spread thin."

"Working at the morgue is only temporary," Randolph said. "Until Wes works off the rest of his community service."

"Right," Wes said. Then he could dedicate his life to golf.

They squinted at him.

Dammit, he'd said that out loud, too.

Coop clapped his hands together. "Let's get measured for the tuxes so I can tell Carlotta to cross it off the list." He signaled a salesclerk.

"Wes," Jack said, pulling him aside. "Can I have a word?"

"Can I say no?"

"No," Jack said with a frown. He looked around to make sure Coop and Randolph were out of earshot. "Dr. Vincent called, wanted to get a restraining order on you. You climbed a damn tree to crawl in his daughter's bedroom window?"

"Yeah."

Jack pulled his hand over his mouth to stifle a grin, then tried to look stern. "Man, you can't do that."

"But I already did."

"You can't do it *again*."

He lifted his chin. "Why not?"

"Cause I gave him my word you wouldn't, that's why. I vouched for you, don't make me look bad."

Wes stabbed at his glasses. "He won't let me see her. It sucks."

"Yeah, I know. But if you really like this girl, you don't want to make an enemy out of her dad."

"Okay," Wes said miserably. "It would help if I could get this damn ankle bracelet off."

Jack grunted. "I'll make a phone call." Then he lifted his finger. "But I can't promise anything."

"Jack," Coop called. "I need my Best Man."

Jack's jaw tightened. "Let's get this over with."

Wes followed him to where Coop and Randolph were trying on jackets. Randolph made eye contact with Wes and raised an eyebrow.

Wes realized he was asking if Jack had quizzed him about Meg's rescue. He gave a small head shake, then raised his arms so the clerk could record his measurements.

Coop was in a jovial mood, and while most men would be counting down their days of freedom, Coop was counting the days until he and Carlotta were married. He joked with the salesclerk and bragged that he'd fallen in love with his bride-to-be at first sight.

"But it took a little longer to convince her," Coop added.

The bell on the door rang. Wes knew it was Carlotta before she came into view simply from the expression on the faces of Coop, Jack, and his dad.

"Hi," she said, looking like a model in a short red dress and strappy sandals. "Don't you all look handsome."

All three men took a half step forward, probably unconsciously. Wes marveled at the way his sister held court, oblivious to her power over all of them.

Him included. His heart jerked sideways when he thought about her happiness—he wanted it for her more than he wanted it for himself. After what she'd endured from him and their parents, she deserved the world. More than anything, he wanted to see her wed to the man of her dreams.

Watching the men respond to her was like studying card players for tells. Coop looked at Carlotta with pure adoration... Randolph looked at her with paternal pride, and Jack looked at her with...

Wes bit down on the inside of his cheek. *Damn.*

CHAPTER 12

ON THE drive to the Reeder house, a news item on the radio caught Carlotta's attention.

"Senator Reeder's family is dealing with another unflattering story this morning. An anonymous woman has come forward saying the Senator's son, Eathan Reeder, made unwanted advances toward her at a political event where she was working as a bartender. A spokesman for the Senator's campaign says it was a misunderstanding in a casual atmosphere and the matter will be handled privately."

Carlotta worked her mouth back and forth. What had Emma Wallace said about the son following in his father's footsteps?

A few minutes later, she pulled up to the gate to the Reeder home, rolled down the window, and spoke into the speaker.

"Carlotta Wren for Mrs. Reeder."

In the ensuing silence, Carlotta's nerves began to bounce. So many things about this situation made her nervous, not the least of which was proximity to the man she suspected had done some terrible things. But she also didn't like the idea of further ingratiating herself to a woman who would undoubtedly be destroyed if her family was torn apart by Carlotta's actions.

"Please pull through the gate," a man's voice said, "and follow the driveway around to the garage."

Carlotta had borrowed Hannah's van to transport the many pieces of clothing she'd acquired for Delinda's approval. She was going to have to consider buying her own van for her business in the near future—the commission from this job would probably be enough for a down payment.

Guilt plucked at her as she pulled the van around to park in front of the garage where Doug directed her. How ethical was it of her to profit from a job she'd taken for ulterior motives?

She turned off the engine and climbed out.

On the other hand, she'd worked overtime to select clothing she thought would accomplish Delinda Reeder's goals... and as Hannah had pointed out, there was the chance that Max Reeder was guilty only of being a consummate flirt. And even if he'd stepped out on his wife, some women looked the other way.

Her mother had when Randolph had carried on with Liz Fischer... although now that she knew more about her parent's relationship, she wondered if Valerie had given Randolph a pass because of her prior relationship that had produced a child Randolph had raised as his own.

She sighed. Relationships were complicated—she should know. Her ups and downs with Peter, Jack, and Coop had intermingled and criss-crossed to the point that at times her heart had felt splintered.

Glancing down at her engagement ring, she smiled, glad those days were behind her.

She enlisted Doug's help to unload two rolling racks and hanging garment bags. Emma emerged from the house and instructed him to use the back entrance to take them to Mrs. Reeder's dressing room. When she turned to Carlotta, her expression seemed pinched. "Delinda is waiting for us, but something unexpected came up and we won't have as much time as we'd hoped."

Did the woman's troubled demeanor and the unexpected business have something to do with the son's alleged indiscretion?

Carlotta nodded. "I understand."

She followed Emma into the house and up the stairs in the direction of Delinda's dressing room. But at the sound of Mrs. Reeder's voice, Emma held up her hand. "Delinda's on the phone. We'll wait."

Carlotta stopped, her ears piqued to catch the bits of conversation that floated out.

"...tired of this... make sure you do..."

Delinda did not sound happy.

"Nice weather we're having," Emma said in an awkward attempt to talk over her boss's conversation.

"Beautiful," Carlotta agreed.

"...just handle it," Delinda said. "Call me back."

When it was clear she'd ended the call, Emma proceeded down the hall. Doug approached from the other direction with the laden clothing racks.

When Carlotta entered, Delinda Reeder was standing near a window, seemingly lost in thought. For the first time, Carlotta thought the woman looked her age. But when she heard them, she turned and gave them all a broad smile. "Hello, Carlotta. Thank you, Doug." She reached out to touch one of the many opaque garment bags. "I can't wait to see what you have for me."

"I can't wait to show you," Carlotta said, then began to unzip and remove the bags.

She'd been able to assemble full outfits on the StyleMe Hangers, complete with accessories. With every reveal, Delinda seemed more delighted.

"These hangers are wonderful," Delinda said. "Where can I buy them?"

"Nowhere yet. My mother is bringing them to market. Consider the hangers a gift for allowing me to test them."

"I informed Carlotta you have another commitment," Emma said.

Delinda's smile slipped a bit. "Yes."

"Let's get started," Carlotta suggested, "and see how far we get."

Helping women try on beautiful clothes never grew old, Carlotta decided as Delinda donned the garments carefully curated for her. Carlotta had covered all the bases, focusing on dresses that could be changed up with a fitted jacket or a great scarf or a statement belt. But she made sure Delinda had lots of pants and skirts to choose from, showing how they could be mixed and matched. For evening wear, she'd chosen luxe separates that could be combined for versatility. For shoes, she'd chosen only styles that would provide comfort during hours of standing, or hurrying from event to event. To Carlotta's delight, Delinda grew more enthusiastic with every outfit change.

"Forget the budget I gave you," Delinda said. "I want to keep everything."

Carlotta smiled wide. "Wonderful."

"We should wrap up soon," Emma murmured.

"Right," Delinda said, her mood sliding—in anticipation of dealing with the situation she'd been discussing on the phone? "Emma, would you fetch Doug to help Carlotta with her supplies?"

Emma glanced at Carlotta—again, with suspicion—then disappeared.

Carlotta began to gather up the garment bags and the few items that hadn't fit. She felt Delinda's gaze on her as she moved.

"Did you enjoy yourself at the fundraiser at the Bedford Manor club?" the woman asked.

"Very much." Had the woman noticed that Max had singled her out for attention?

"I know now why you seemed so familiar to me," Delinda said.

Carlotta managed an innocent expression. "Oh?"

"I ran into Adele Ashford at the fundraiser and she complimented my dress. When I mentioned your name..." Delinda smiled. "Let's just say she had some interesting things to say about you and your family."

Carlotta wet her lips. "I used to date Peter, but I ended things a while ago, and his mother feels as though I abandoned him."

"A terrible shame what happened to him," Delinda said. "Max was prepared to put in a good word for his bail hearing."

"I know," Carlotta said. "I wish the Senator had gotten the chance. Peter didn't deserve what happened to him." She pressed her lips together. "As for my family's reputation—"

"I assume it was a mother's grief talking," Delinda cut in graciously. "Besides, we can't help what the members of our family do, can we?"

The way the woman said it made her think she was referring to her husband's—and son's--alleged misdeeds. "No," Carlotta agreed, busying herself with the bags. She chose her words carefully. "Your family has certainly been under a great deal of scrutiny lately."

Delinda sighed. "Yes. That unfortunate incident with the Mason woman... what a tragedy. She was a sad, confused person. But being in the public spotlight, Max is bound to attract female attention." She dimpled like a coed. "He is handsome, if I do say so."

Carlotta smiled. "Yes, he is."

The woman nodded to Carlotta's left hand. "I see you found love again."

"Yes. In fact, I'm getting married in a few weeks."

"Oh, how lovely. I'll bet your dress is spectacular."

Carlotta pressed her lips together. The mystery dress Jarold Jett had promised her still hadn't arrived. "I hope everyone thinks so," she hedged.

"In my practice, a good majority of my clients are brides-to-be, wanting fillers or Botox to look their best for their wedding photos."

"Do you still practice medicine?" Carlotta asked.

"Another physician in the practice is covering my patients while I focus on the campaign." She angled her head. "You don't need it, but I could give you a touch here and there if you want to look... refreshed."

Carlotta bit into her lip and glanced into a nearby mirror as she walked by. Did she need it? "Thank you. I'll think about it."

Delinda reached into her open closet to touch the sleeve of the blue caped dress she'd worn to the fundraiser. "This outfit was quite a hit," Delinda said. "Emma said our social media numbers went up when pictures from the evening were posted."

"That's wonderful to hear."

Delinda frowned. "Ugh, Max's hair—the man sheds like a dog sometimes."

Carlotta perked up. Hair? Maybe she could get a DNA sample to compare to the fluid in the condom in her freezer.

"Allow me." She reached into her bag to remove a roll-over lint remover. She rolled it over the caped dress, her pulse bumping higher to see dark hairs sticking to the surface. With a smile, she replaced the roller's cover, then returned it to her bag.

"There's another event tomorrow evening, if you'd like to attend," Delinda said. "It's for a city councilman, so it'll be a different crowd than was at Bedford Manor."

Meaning the Ashfords wouldn't be there.

And it would give her a chance to wear another one of Lolly Day's designs.

"I'd love to, thank you."

Emma returned with Doug in tow.

Delinda walked toward the door. "Thank you, Carlotta, for all your hard work."

"I enjoyed every minute."

"Emma, please give Carlotta tickets to tomorrow's event."

Emma gave a curt nod. Delinda waved, then disappeared down a hallway, walking rapidly.

While Doug went in the opposite direction with the racks, Emma escorted Carlotta back to the van and handed over the event tickets.

"I suppose I'll see you there," Emma said.

"Thank you for your help again today."

Emma's mouth quirked. "Like I said, it's my job. Goodbye."

Carlotta opened the van doors for Doug to reload her supplies. She thanked him, then hurriedly climbed in to start the van. She could hardly wait to get home to study the hairs from the roller with a magnifying glass. With luck, they would have a root for DNA extraction.

Then when Jack asked for the evidence she'd been stockpiling regarding Patricia's case, she could add the hairs to the mix.

On the way back to the townhome, she listened to the news for more information about the Eathan Reeder incident, but the media seemed to have moved on.

Or, more likely, the story had already been squashed by the Reeders' team.

When she reached the townhome, she jogged inside to her office and found her magnifying glass in her desk drawer. Her heartbeat raced as she withdrew the sticky lint roller, then scrutinized the two dark hairs belonging to Max Reeder.

No roots.

Her shoulders fell. Darn.

Which meant she'd have to find a way to get his DNA at tomorrow's event.

CHAPTER 13

"WHAT A lovely dress."

Carlotta smiled at the woman next to her in the bar line and angled her body to best show off the turquoise halter dress. Long ties ending in silver beaded tassels hung down her back. "Thank you. The designer is Lolly Day. She's local, you should look her up."

"I will."

"Are you a supporter of Senator Reeder's?" Carlotta asked.

"I'm here to support Councilwoman Thomas," the woman said, taking her drink from the bartender. "But the fact that she's aligned with Max Reeder makes me inclined to vote for him."

Carlotta gave her another smile, then stepped up to order white wine. She preferred red, but not while wearing borrowed clothing.

While she waited for her drink, she glanced around the warehouse-sized art gallery housing the event. A silent auction throughout the evening was the main fundraiser, although she suspected the admission tickets hadn't been cheap. The attendees were definitely more youthful as was to be expected in the trendy venue.

The Reeders had already arrived and were doing media interviews and posing for photographs with local council members in a far corner. Delinda was radiant in one of the new dresses Carlotta had selected for her in bright coral. Max's booming laugh carried across the noise of the crowd. The man was in his element in front of an audience, she acknowledged—he seemed born to be admired.

"White wine," the bartender said with a smile, extending her glass. "That'll be ten dollars."

"I got this." Jack reached past her to hand the man a twenty. "And I'll take a beer."

Carlotta attributed the uptick in her pulse to surprise. "Jack... what are you doing here?"

"Schmoozing," he said sourly. "Part of the new job duties."

She smiled at his attire—his best suit. She knew because she'd made him buy it on a shopping trip after his promotion. "At least you look the part."

"Don't rub it in." He waved aside the glass the bartender offered and took the bottle. They walked away a few feet. "What are you doing here?"

"Business," she said, indicating her dress. "I'm a brand representative now."

"Come again?"

"I get paid to wear clothes to parties."

Jack smiled as he lifted the bottle of beer for a drink. "That's a thing?"

"Yes, Jack." She took a drink of the wine. "I guess you haven't had a chance to stop by to get the boxes of evidence I have from Patricia's hotel room."

His mouth flattened. "I'm still thinking about it."

She arched an eyebrow. "Or maybe you came tonight to get a bead on Max Reeder."

The muscle that worked in his jaw told her she was right. "I could say the same thing about you... although I hope you know better."

She flapped her eyelashes. "I'm just here to look good, Jack."

He raked his gaze over her, head to toe, but swallowed whatever he might have said with a drink of his beer. He glanced all around. "Where's your partner?"

"Hannah was busy—she mukbangs for money now."

"I don't even want to know what that is. And I was talking about Coop."

"Oh." Her cheeks warmed. She hadn't asked Coop because she planned to chat up the Senator tonight and knew it would be easier without her fiancé at her side. "He was busy, too."

Jack's eyebrow twitched. "Ah."

It occurred to her that Jack might also watch her like a hawk. She needed to establish some distance, i.e., irritate him. "Are you close to making an arrest for Peter's murder?"

"No." He took another drink of beer.

"Do you think Walt Tully is behind it?"

"I'm not ruling it out," he said finally, "but short of a confession from Walt or the man who did it, we got nothing. You really need to stop dwelling on it, Carlotta."

"Are you putting pressure on the inmates?"

He sighed. "The D.A. is offering incentives for information, but nothing has come of it." He gestured to the room of pretty people. "I guess I'm supposed to network a little, so I should probably make the rounds."

She smiled into her drink. "Later, Jack."

He strolled away with the body language of a bear whose leg was caught in a trap. She took another drink of wine and assessed the room. The Senator had left the media area and was perusing the silent auction table with a couple of suited men she recognized as council members. The men were focused on the art, but the Senator kept looking up and scanning.

Carlotta stepped into his line of sight and he stopped. Pretending not to notice, she walked a circuitous route to a side entrance where she'd noticed smokers coming and going surreptitiously. The Senator was a reported closet smoker, and yesterday when she'd been lint-rolling Delinda's dress, she'd caught a faint whiff of cigarette smoke—secondhand?

She abandoned her drink on a table and slipped out the side door, leaving it ajar. Outside, a well-dressed man was smoking in the dim light of a streetlamp, but when he saw her, he took a quick drag, then dropped it and squashed it under his foot before walking back inside.

It seemed no one associated with politics these days wanted to be caught indulging in the dirty little vice.

She reached into her purse and pulled out an unlit cigarette. It felt good between her fingers. Her pulse quickened with the anticipation of incoming nicotine. She was literally playing with fire, she knew, because she'd worked hard to kick the habit, and smoking just one could start it all up again.

The door scraped open and she looked up to see Max Reeder slip outside. He saw her and smiled, then pushed the door closed. Her heart raced as he walked closer, hands in pockets, so cool and casual.

"Hi," he said. "We meet again."

"Yes, we do." She put the cigarette in her mouth, then pretended to rummage for a light.

"Got another one of those?" he asked.

"You smoke?"

"Occasionally," he said, then grinned. "Don't tell my wife."

"It'll be our secret," she said, handing him a cigarette. To her surprise, he withdrew a lighter from his pocket and flicked it alive. He lit his cigarette with a puff, then offered to light hers.

She hesitated, then leaned over to put the tip of the cigarette in the blue flame, and inhaled.

It. Tasted. So. Good. Her lungs began to sing with addiction recall. She moaned with enjoyment.

"I know, right?" he said, drawing deeply on his. "Sometimes it just feels so good."

She took another draw, then exhaled and gave him a coy look. "So... do you keep other things from your wife?"

He laughed, then looked her up and down and flicked ash. "Only with other people who can keep things from my wife."

She angled her head. "I already signed a non-disclosure agreement."

He gave a little growl and leaned his head close. "Well then, what are we waiting for?"

The door opened abruptly, and the man straightened to put distance between them. They turned their heads to see who'd emerged. Carlotta was taking a deep draw, but when she saw it was Jack, she choked and launched into a coughing fit.

Max took a big step away from her toward Jack, smiling and extending his hand. "I'm Max Reeder."

He was a pro, she acknowledged... the key to not arousing suspicion was to act as if nothing was amiss.

"Jack Terry," Jack said pleasantly, pumping his hand.

"Nice to know you, Jack."

"I'm Carlotta," she said, offering her hand to Jack.

Jack's jaw hardened, but he clasped her hand. "Carlotta." But he held on longer than necessary, and gave her a warning squeeze.

"We were just having a quick puff," Max said. "Nasty habit, please don't tell my wife." The Senator laughed, then waited for Jack to confirm.

"Tell her what?" Jack asked. "I didn't see a thing."

"Good man," Max said with a grin. "I guess I'd better get back inside."

He started to toss down his cigarette, but Carlotta stopped him. "I'll finish it." She smiled. "They're so expensive."

"Right," Max said, handing her the half-smoked butt. "Hope to see you both at the polls."

"Sure thing," Jack said, but after Max walked by him, Jack kept his gaze on her.

When the door closed behind the Senator, Jack exploded. "What the hell are you up to?"

"Nothing," Carlotta lied.

He scowled. "I thought you quit smoking."

She shrugged. "I did... but I guess the stress of the wedding is getting to me." She snubbed out both cigarettes against a metal post and started to return them to her purse.

"Freeze."

She looked up, expecting to see him holding a gun on her. "What, Jack?"

"I know what you're doing, or what you *think* you're doing."

She scoffed. "What am I doing?"

He walked closer. "You're trying to get the Senator's DNA to match to the condom you picked up in the hotel bathroom."

Instead of denying it, she frowned. "If you'd do your job, then I wouldn't have to be skulking around in a parking lot with Senator Glad Hands."

His mouth tightened, then he gestured to the two cigarettes. "Okay... which one is his?"

She handed over the cigarette.

Jack took a few steps, dropped the butt into a puddle of oily water, then ground it under his heel.

"Jack! Now it's useless as evidence."

"It was useless before," Jack said. "Because there's no chain of custody. *Stop* playing detective, Carlotta."

She sighed and changed tack. "Okay, but tell me you'll at least get the security footage from the hotel the night Patricia died. It might reveal something. And if it doesn't, I'll let this go."

He closed his eyes briefly. "I'll make a call, but after all this time, it's probably not available."

"Maybe so," she agreed.

Jack gestured to the door. "Are you going back inside?"

"Go ahead," she said, holding up the other butt. "I think I'll finish this."

"Then I'm taking off," he said.

"Okay. Goodnight, Jack." She gave him a little wave, laughing to herself when he stomped back to the door, then opened and closed it with more force than necessary.

Carlotta looked back to the butt she held and smiled as she dropped it into a plastic baggie. *This* was the butt Senator Reeder had been smoking—the one she'd given to Jack had been hers.

CHAPTER 14

"AFTER WE break ground on the golf course," Randolph said, "we should start planning our first tournament. They're cash cows."

"Sounds good," Wes said.

He was sick to death of hearing about plans for the Wren & Son Golf Center, but he gave his dad a pass because he was trying to kill time while they waited in the lobby of the courtroom to be called. His knee jumped with nerves. The judge would rule on whether he'd violated probation when he'd cut off his ankle monitor. The penalty ranged anywhere from having to wear the damn thing even longer to being thrown in jail. His attorney had told him it depended on the judge they drew and what mood the judge was in.

He put his hand to his mouth to chew a nail, then remembered he'd quit that nasty habit and shoved his hand under his jumping leg.

If he went to jail, he could say goodbye to the chance of seeing Meg again. Ironic considering he'd cut off the ankle monitor when he'd been planning to hop a plane to Europe to look for her.

With a fake passport, but no one needed to know that part.

"Try to relax," Randolph said. "The judge needs to see a young man who's confident and has a future ahead of him."

Great—because he had no confidence and his future was watching people try to put a stupid little ball into a stupid little hole.

Wes looked up to see his attorney, Joe Forrest, beckoning him forward. "Judge Hondo is ready for us."

Wes and Randolph stood. "What kind of judge is Hondo?" his dad asked.

The man gave the thumbs down. "Old school hard ass. Tough break. I'll do the best I can."

Dread filled Wes's stomach and leadened his feet. He buttoned the jacket to his suit and trudged into the courtroom. The sight of his probation officer Eldora Jones sitting in the rear of the room gave him a little lift. She flashed an encouraging smile, and he tried to smile back. Randolph took a seat in the gallery. Wes followed his attorney to the front of the room and took a seat behind a heavy wood table. Across from them a young female A.D.A. stood at a table, reviewing his file.

It was thick.

Wes leaned close to Forrest. "Don't forget to ask the judge to rescind the part of my probation from the hacking charge that prevents me from having a computer in the house."

"You're pushing it, kid."

Wes frowned. "I need one, and so does my sister, for her business."

His attorney turned his head. "Oh, shit."

Wes followed his line of sight to see D.A. Kelvin Lucas shuffle into the room. The toady man had prosecuted Randolph when he'd first been charged with investment fraud, and had taken it personally when Randolph had skipped town. Lucas had pressured Carlotta to try to smoke out their parents by threatening to prosecute Wes's computer break-in to the fullest extent, and had pulled other strings to generally make their lives miserable.

Lucas and Randolph exchanged contentious nods. When Randolph had returned to Atlanta and not only been exonerated of former charges but had helped to take down the real criminals at Mashburn & Tully, Lucas was left in the awkward juncture of embarrassment and appreciation.

Who knew how he felt about the Wrens now?

"Why is he here?" Wes asked.

"It looks as if the D.A. has taken a personal interest in your hearing," Forrest muttered.

Wes closed his eyes… he was fucked.

"All rise," the bailiff announced.

Wes pushed to his feet and tried to get a read on the judge when he walked in. If the man's scowl was any indication, he was having a bad year.

"Be seated," Judge Hondo bellowed, falling heavily into his seat. He looked over his bench and arched a bushy eyebrow. "D.A. Lucas, to what do I owe the honor?"

Kelvin Lucas gave a little smile. "Just following through on a couple of early charges my office filed."

The Judge looked at his docket. "That would be charges against Wesley Wren?"

"Correct, Your Honor."

Judge Hondo looked toward Wes. "Are you Wesley Wren?"

"Yes," Wes said.

Forrest elbowed him.

"Sir," Wes added. "Your Honor, sir."

"Why are we here today, counselors?"

Forrest began to speak, but Lucas edged him out. "To decide if Mr. Wren violated probation when he removed his ankle monitor."

The judge looked perplexed. "Is there ever a legitimate reason for a defendant to remove an ankle monitor?"

"Joe Forrest for the defendant," Wes's attorney offered. "Mr. Wren had worn the ankle monitor for the time prescribed in his probation agreement, but—" He coughed. "Because my schedule was overbooked, I couldn't find time to attend a hearing to have it removed."

Actually, his father had told Forrest to stall because the ankle bracelet was the only thing keeping him Stateside when Meg was missing.

The Judge gave Wes a flat smile. "So you took it upon yourself to remove it?"

"Yes, Your Honor, for a good reason."

The Judge looked dubious. "Let me guess—a girl?"

Wes's shoulders fell. "Yeah... Your Honor."

The gallery tittered.

"The bracelet was off for a matter of hours," his attorney said. "We contend there was no violation of probation and are asking that it be removed so Mr. Wren can more easily complete his court-ordered community service with the county morgue."

Kelvin Lucas cleared his throat. "The original charges were serious, Your Honor. Fraud and passing counterfeit bills."

"Federal?" Judge Hondo said. "Why isn't he in jail?"

Wes's stomach cramped.

"There were extenuating circumstances," Lucas said. "Mr. Wren's crime revealed a larger crime organization which allowed the government to offer leniency in sentencing."

"Is Mr. Wren fulfilling other obligations of his probation?"

"Yes, Your Honor," Forrest said, then held up a sheet of paper. "An affidavit from Mr. Wren's probation officer saying he's kept all his appointments and passed random drug tests."

"And you've stayed out of trouble?" the judge asked Wes.

He opened his mouth to say yes, mostly, but was cut off by a man's voice from the rear of the room.

"Your Honor, may I approach the bench?"

Wes turned his head to see Jack standing in the back of the gallery.

"Detective Jack Terry," the judge said with a little smile. "Do you have a dog in this fight?"

"You might say that," Jack said. "I'd like to vouch for Mr. Wren."

Hondo glanced at papers in front of him. "This says you were the arresting officer when Mr. Wren was charged in hacking into the records of this courthouse."

"That's correct, Your Honor. He was given probation."

"Then graduated to counterfeiting and fraud."

Jack inclined his head in concession. "Wes has made a few mistakes, but he's a good young man with a bright future. If he does something to violate probation, I'll personally bring him in."

The judge pursed his mouth. "You have an impressive champion here, Mr. Wren." He looked at Lucas. "Is this young man a danger to society?"

Lucas turned to glance at Wes, then at Randolph, before turning back with a defeated expression. "No, sir, the state doesn't believe so." He frowned. "We won't object to Mr. Wren's monitoring device being removed."

Hondo gave them all a flat smile. "Oh, happy day, we're all in agreement."

Hope bubbled in Wes's chest—things were going his way? He bumped his attorney's arm. "Don't forget."

"You should quit while you're ahead," Forrest murmured.

"Do it, or I will."

The man's mouth tightened. "Your Honor, there's one more thing. Under the terms of Mr. Wren's probation in the hacking charge, he was forbidden to have computer equipment in the home where he resides. We ask for that part of the probation agreement to be set aside."

The judge narrowed his eyes at Wes. "So you can hack my courthouse records again, young man?"

"No, Your Honor," Wes said. "I need a computer… for college." He could almost feel his father bristle behind him.

"You're enrolled in college?"

"Not yet, sir. But I'm getting ready to take the entrance exam. I want to be a doctor." Wes straightened. "I mean, I'm *going* to be a doctor."

The judge studied him and Wes wondered what the man saw—a skinny little punk with big dreams and no game?

Hondo's mouth turned into something that resembled a smile. "I believe you will, Mr. Wren." He looked back to his papers. "Let the record show the court is ordering that Mr. Wren's ankle monitor be removed immediately—bailiff, please do that now—and the prohibition on Mr. Wren using computer equipment is waived. Next case."

Wes fist-pumped the air. The bailiff walked over and leaned down, then used a tool to remove the ankle monitor. Wes felt as if a shackle had been cut off.

He could do anything now.

When he turned, the first person he saw was his dad. Randolph gave him a wry smile, then nodded toward the lobby. "I'll meet you out there."

After signing a few papers, Wes and his attorney left the courtroom. When they reached the lobby, Forrest wheeled off in another direction. In the sea of milling bodies, a hand waved. Eldora and Jack stood waiting for him. Wes strode up, unable to keep the grin off his face.

"Congrats," she said. "I have to go, but I wanted to say you did good in there."

"Thanks for coming, E. See you next week?"

"Actually, I'm recommending that you drop back to checking in once a month."

His grin diminished. "Really?" He realized it was a good thing, but he would miss seeing her as often.

"Take care, Wes."

She walked away and Jack gave him a little smile. "Feel better?"

"You have no idea." Wes wet his lips. "Hey, man, thanks for what you said in there."

Jack nodded. "I meant it."

"That I have a bright future?"

"And if you do anything to violate probation, I'll personally bring you in."

Wes frowned. "Have you seen my dad?"

"Yeah, he said to tell you he'll pick you up out front. See you around?"

Wes nodded, then watched the detective stride away. When had he stopped hating the big man?

When he turned toward the front entrance, a knot formed in his stomach. Randolph had told him before that college wasn't for him, that he was already behind others his age, that medical school would take too long, cost too much, and that medicine wouldn't pay as well as going into business.

And he was probably right.

He walked outside and spotted his dad's SUV coming around. When he opened the door and climbed inside, his gaze landed on the new box of business cards for the Wren & Son Golf Center sitting in the middle of the console.

Before he lost his nerve, he opened his mouth and forced the words past a tight throat. "Dad... I didn't mean to blindside you in there about going to college. I don't expect you to pay for it. And I'll work whatever hours you need me at the golf center."

Randolph gave him a sad little smile. "But you don't want to run the business with me?"

Wes shook his head. "No. But Chance does... and he's good at it. I know he can be frustrating, but he has a big heart, and he has a kid on the way. He wants to prove himself."

His dad seemed to be considering his words as he drove. Sweat beaded on Wes's lip in the extended silence. More than anything, he wanted Randolph to be proud of him. Maybe he should've waited until he'd taken the SAT before mouthing off about being a doctor. Meg's father's words came back to him. *Boy, you probably couldn't even pass the college entrance exam.*

Wes closed his eyes. What was the point of trying? He'd failed at everything he'd ever attempted.

He realized the SUV had stopped. When he opened his eyes, he saw the sign for a big box electronics store. "Why are we here?"

"If you're going to go to college," Randolph said, "you're going to need a computer with all the bells and whistles." His dad reached over to touch his arm. "I'm proud of you, son, for knowing what you want to do with your life, and for going after it. I'll support you all I can."

A lump of emotion formed in the back of Wes's throat. He swallowed hard and managed a smile. "Thanks, Dad."

CHAPTER 15

CARLOTTA PARKED the Miata in the lot for the county morgue. She flashed back in her mind to the first time she'd visited the building with Hannah and Jolie Goodman to identify a body. She remembered wondering how anyone could work at such a morbid place. Now two of the men she loved most worked there, and she knew her way around the place pretty well.

She checked in at the front desk. "Dr. Craft is expecting me."

The receptionist consulted a schedule. "Dr. Craft is in the lab on the fourth floor. I'll let him know you're on your way."

Carlotta walked to the elevator, feeling antsy about what she was about to ask Coop to do. But in this case, she rationalized, the end justified the means. On the other hand, keeping him in the dark about what he actually would be doing was probably best to protect him professionally.

When she stepped off the elevator, she was pleased to see Wes dressed in a white lab coat pushing a cart of supplies.

"Hi, stranger. I haven't seen much of you lately."

His smile was uncharacteristic. "Hi, Sis. You here to see Coop?"

She held up some travel brochures. "We're planning our honeymoon. But I was hoping to run into you. Mom told me you had a good day in court yesterday."

He pulled up his pant leg and grinned. "Got rid of the bracelet."

"That's great. And I hear you're going to take the college entrance exam?"

Wes blushed. "Yeah, I have to take it in a couple of weeks in order to apply for the fall term."

"That's quick, will you have time to prepare?"

"I'm studying every spare minute at the golf center and when I have downtime here. And Dad bought me a sweet computer setup, I'll pick it up tomorrow."

She took in the young man before her, marveling that not long ago she was worried he wouldn't make it to adulthood. "I'm so proud of you." She leaned forward to give him a hug and for once, he didn't object. Before she got too misty, she released him. "How is Meg?"

Wes shrugged. "Getting better, I think. I, um... haven't talked to her for a while. I've been so busy."

She could tell there was more to the story, but she knew better than to press.

"I should get back to work," he said, nodding to the cart. "See you at home."

Home. The word hit her hard as she turned toward the lab. Since their parents had left, home for her and Wes had been the townhouse, and while she assumed she'd move into Coop's industrial condo, she hadn't considered how much the move would affect her and Wes. For so long it had been just the two of them...

What was it Hannah had said? That everything was changing.

"Brides-to-be are supposed to be happy," Coop chided.

She looked up to see him standing in the doorway. She smiled. "I am, silly, just deep in thought."

"About?"

"Am I moving into your place after the wedding?"

He blinked. "Of course. My home is your home. That's okay, isn't it?"

"Yeah, it's just we haven't really talked about it."

"That's because when we start talking, you distract me."

She smiled and met him halfway for a juicy kiss.

He grunted and shifted. "See what I mean."

Carlotta laughed. "Are you busy today?"

He waved her into the lab furnished with stainless tables studded with equipment, and glass-fronted cabinets full of chemicals. "No more than usual, I have a few minutes."

She pulled the travel brochures from her bag. "I picked up these brochures at the mall. Want to take a look when you get a moment?"

He glanced over them. "Paris, London, Milan. Hm… fashion capitals of the world."

She bit into her lip. "You figured me out."

Coop laughed. "I will take you anywhere you want to go." He dipped his chin. "As long as I get to dress and undress you."

Warmth flooded her cheeks. "You will." She wet her lips and tried to inject a casual note into her voice. "And while I'm here, I need a favor."

"Uh-oh. I know that voice."

"What voice?" she asked innocently.

"That voice that means you're going to ask me to do something I shouldn't, and I'm going to do it because I can't resist making you happy."

She grinned. "Really?"

He tried to look stern. "What's the favor?"

She removed two baggies from her purse and set them on a nearby lab table. "Can you run DNA on these two items to see if they're a match?"

He glanced at the baggies. "A cigarette, and what's in the other bag?"

"It's, um, a… condom. Used."

He winced. "Does this have something to do with the friend of yours who wanted to rehydrate semen to do a paternity test?"

"You remember that."

"I do," he said, referring to when he'd unwittingly revealed how she could prepare a sample of the semen to send off for DNA testing.

Carlotta chose her words carefully. "Isn't it easier to test two items to see if they match than to do a paternity test?"

"If the baby hasn't been born, sure."

"Good," she said. "And thank you." She leaned forward and kissed him, releasing some of her pent up stress. The man was a lovely kisser, and she was regretting their pact to wait until their wedding night to have sex again. He moaned into her mouth, conveying he, too, was straining under their agreement.

The sound of someone clearing their throat reached them.

Carlotta turned her head to see Jack standing in the doorway of the lab. He gave a little wave. "Sorry to interrupt."

"I was just leaving," Carlotta offered.

Jack spied the baggies on the table and walked closer to examine them.

Carlotta closed her eyes and swallowed a curse. When she opened her eyes, Jack looked as if he was going to ignite. "You gave me the wrong cigarette, didn't you?"

She decided not to respond.

"What's he talking about?" Coop asked.

She was still mulling her choices, and when she didn't respond right away, Coop looked back to Jack.

"Clue me in?"

Jack arched an eyebrow in her direction. "Coop doesn't know what you're up to with all this business about Patricia Alexander's death?"

Coop looked back to her. "I thought you were done with all that."

"Oh, no," Jack said, walking closer. "She's not done. In fact, she's accumulating DNA samples to support a cockamamie theory she pieced together in which Max Reeder is apparently a serial killer."

"Senator Max Reeder?" Coop asked.

"I didn't say he was a serial killer," she corrected. "But he could be involved in Patricia's death... and the death of Colleen Mason."

Coop frowned. "The local woman who committed suicide?"

"Allegedly," she said.

Jack looked at Coop as if to say, 'See what I mean?'

Carlotta defiantly explained her swapped makeup cases theory to Coop. "I think the condom was in the Mason woman's bag and it fell out when someone came to Patricia's hotel room to swap it back."

Coop pointed to a baggie. "This condom?"

"That Carlotta lifted from the hotel bathroom," Jack supplied dryly.

"What's the source of the cigarette?" Coop asked, pointing to the other baggie.

Jack coughed. "Carlotta lured the Senator out for a smoke the other night at a party."

Coop turned a frown her way. "I thought you quit smoking."

She sighed, exasperated with both of them. "You're both standing there looking at me as if I'm crazy, when all you have to do is test the DNA from both and we'll know if I'm on the right track."

"Carlotta, you can go around playing Nancy Drew," Jack said in an irritated tone, "but Coop and I have to adhere to protocol."

Carlotta crossed her arms and glared at him. "Why are you here, Jack?"

His mouth morphed into a wry smile. "I thought it was time to plan the bachelor party. That's one of the Best Man's responsibilities."

Her mouth tightened, then she plucked the two baggies off the table and dropped them in her purse. "Coop," she said sweetly, "call me when you've had a chance to go over the brochures so we can plan our honeymoon."

She turned and left the lab, fuming.

Why wouldn't they listen to her?

CHAPTER 16

CARLOTTA OPENED the door to Moody's cigar bar and immediately, her mood lifted. Long ago when she'd found a premium cigar in the returned jacket of a customer who'd turned up dead, she'd walked into Moody's to do research and had wound up bonding with the owner of the retro bar reminiscent of a 1920s speakeasy. Happy hour was winding down, so the bar wasn't as crowded as usual. The murmur of conversation over lounge music provided a pleasant background for socializing or for drinking alone.

June Moody herself was wiping down the top of the large horseshoe-shaped bar that served up signature cocktails, plus cigars and loose tobacco from the cabinets that lined the walls and from bar-top humidors. When she glanced up, she stopped and smiled wide. "Hi, Carlotta."

Carlotta slid onto a stool at the bar. "Hi, June. How have you been?"

"Not as good as you. I received the wedding invitation—congratulations."

"Thanks."

"Let me see that ring."

She extended her left hand, taking the moment to enjoy the beauty of the custom diamond.

"Gorgeous," June said. "Coop has such good taste."

She nodded and smiled. "Everything about the man is good."

June laughed. "You two make such a nice couple. I couldn't be happier for you."

"Will you be able to attend the wedding?"

"Wouldn't miss it. I already dropped my RSVP back in the mail."

Guilt stabbed Carlotta when she visualized the stack of RSVPs on her desk that she hadn't yet opened. There were just so many details to tend to.

"Are you meeting Coop here?"

"Um, no… Rainie Stephens."

June arched an eyebrow. "Coop's former girlfriend? This should be interesting."

"They weren't serious," Carlotta offered. "And Rainie is engaged now."

"I think it's nice you can be friends."

Like Jack and Coop, Carlotta mused.

"What can I get you to drink?" June asked.

"Surprise me."

"And would you like a cigar?"

Since she'd sampled the cigarette at the party where she'd conspired to get Max Reeder's DNA, her cravings had returned to dog her. "I'd better not," she said, shaking her head.

"Let me know if you change your mind. I'll be right back with your drink." June went to ring up another customer, giving Carlotta a chance to people-watch. The crowd that gravitated to Moody's was eclectic and prosperous. She'd run into Peter here more than once with his group of yuppie friends.

The memory of him squeezed her heart. He was a decent man who'd been raised with privilege. His life—pretty Buckhead wife, country club membership, white-collar job—had been pre-destined before he was old enough to make his own decisions.

Like Tracey Tully Lowenstein.

And like her life would've been if Randolph hadn't been caught up in the scandal that had triggered her parents to leave town.

When she'd taken the fantastical trip to another place while under the influence of painkillers, she'd gotten a sense of what it would've been like to be married to Peter and live the life he'd lived, and it hadn't been all she'd thought it would be. She suspected Peter would agree and if given the chance, might've made different decisions with his life going forward.

Except he'd never get that chance. And his death had been chalked up to a random act of violence in jail. That kind of tragedy she could learn to live with... but the thought of someone ordering him to be killed...

"Sidecar Punch," June said, setting a yellow-colored drink in front of her. "It's strong, so pace yourself."

"Thanks," Carlotta said, tasting the sweet, tart drink. "Mm, that's good."

"Thanks for saving me a seat," Rainie said, sliding onto the stool next to her. The curvy redhead had a ready smile. "Hi, June."

"Hi, Rainie. What can I get for you to drink?"

"I'll have a Paris Three Way," she said with a wink.

June laughed and Carlotta relented with a smile. "Did you have to go there?"

"Elephant in the room," Rainie said. "Hey, it's not like we're going to compare notes on Coop's performance... are we?"

Carlotta coughed. "No, we are not."

"Fine with me," Rainie said, then she sighed. "Although I do miss that part of our relationship."

Carlotta gave a little laugh, but unreasonable jealousy sparked in her chest. She and Coop were certainly compatible between the sheets, and she was sure it would only get better. "Tell me about your fiancé."

"Dennis is a dentist."

She blinked at the abbreviation description. "And?"

"And that's about it," Rainie said cheerfully. "He's a super guy and he'll be a terrific dad one day. I could do a lot worse."

Carlotta was a little dismayed at the clinical way the woman summed up her intended life partner, but everyone had different expectations.

"How are your wedding plans coming along?" Rainie asked. "You don't have much time, you must be getting excited."

"Right," Carlotta said. "Things are... falling into place... I think. We have a great venue, so that's most of it."

"The Georgian Terrace is beautiful," Rainie agreed. "We looked there, but it wasn't available for the date we wanted. What's your dress like?"

"Um... I don't have one yet."

Rainie's eyes widened. "Gosh, Carlotta, don't wait until the last minute. It took me months to find a dress—it's a Vera Wang—and I've had to endure two fittings."

"A designer friend is shipping a dress. I'm just hoping it'll be... suitable."

"Wow, that's a gamble."

"Uh-huh." Carlotta lifted her glass for another drink and searched for another subject. "Hannah is putting together a bachelorette party to have here at Moody's upstairs in the lounge. Would you like to come?"

"Sure. Is it a Botox party?"

Carlotta squinted. "What's that?"

"Lots of brides are having Botox parties, you know, to get everyone ready for the photos."

Carlotta touched her face, remembering Delinda Reeder's offer. "I'll mention it to Hannah."

"Where are you going on your honeymoon?"

"We haven't decided yet, maybe London."

"Oh, nice. Coop is great to travel with."

Carlotta schooled her face to mask her surprise. The only trip she and Coop had taken was a road trip for a body haul, and Wes had tagged along. "Coop is so easy-going, he'd make any vacation fun." And when she and Coop were in Vegas at the same time, she'd been engaged to Peter. Setting aside June's advice, she lifted her glass for a hearty drink. "Rainie, have you heard anything else about Peter's attack?"

The woman's mouth went flat and she avoided eye contact. "No."

"Rainie?"

She sighed. "Maybe, but I really can't say anything yet. Just know that Jack Terry is working on it."

Carlotta lifted an eyebrow. "Jack?"

"But you did not hear that from me."

"Here you are," June said, setting Rainie's drink in front of her. "You brides let me know if you need anything else."

Carlotta leaned forward. "Actually, I think I'll have a cigar after all—a Juliet."

"Coming right up."

When June turned away, Rainie lifted her glass. "To happily ever after."

Carlotta clinked her glass to Rainie's. "To happily ever after."

CHAPTER 17

WES RUBBED his gritty eyes, then read aloud the test question for the third time.

"The gas mileage for Neil's station wagon is 17 miles per gallon when the car travels at an average speed of 52 miles per hour. The car's gas tank has 12 gallons of gas at the beginning of a trip. If Neil's car travels at average speed, which of the following functions (*f*) models the number of gallons of gas remaining in the tank (*t*) at the beginning of the trip?"

He looked over the list of four equations to choose from, one as mystifying as the next. He grunted. "Why don't you drive off a cliff, Neil?"

He'd gotten straight A's in Algebra in high school, but apparently he'd forgotten everything since. Maybe his short addiction to Oxy had killed enough brain cells to lower his I.Q.

"How's it going?" Chance asked, strolling up to the vending machine in the golf center's break room.

Wes snapped the SAT study book closed. "Okay, I guess."

"Dude, med school sounds, like, impossible. I barely got my associates degree."

"*We* barely got your associates degree," Wes reminded him. Chance had paid him to take most of his exams.

"I don't know how you can keep all that smart stuff in your head."

He hadn't. A panicky feeling had imbedded itself in his stomach. He was in over his head, and Meg's father's laughing declaration kept knifing through his inadequate brain.

Boy, you probably couldn't even pass the college entrance exam.

Maybe he should've stuck with playing cards, worked his way back up in the local clubs.

The side door opened and Randolph thrust his head inside. "Chance, why don't you and I get some lunch?"

Chance pointed to the vending machine. "I was gonna get a pop and a couple of bags of Doritos. Want one?"

Randolph gave him a flat smile. "I'm inviting you to have lunch with me."

Chance's eyes boinged wide. "Really?"

"Really. I thought we could talk business, if Wes doesn't mind covering things until we get back."

Wes shook his head. "I don't mind."

Chance looked like a kid invited to hang out with Santa Claus. "Sure thing, Mr. W. Can I take a dump first?"

Wes swallowed a laugh.

"Sure," Randolph said. "I'll wait in the car."

"Hope you have air freshener," Chance called as he headed toward the bathroom.

Randolph shot Wes a dubious look. "I hope you're right about him."

"I am. Give him a chance."

"How's the studying going?"

Wes managed a smile. "Good. The study software on the computer is awesome." Except he kept getting distracted with video poker.

"Great. I'm sure you'll ace the test, son. We'll be back in a couple of hours."

Wes maintained his smile until Randolph was out of sight, then he opened the SAT study book again and reread the math problem. One of the equations seemed to make more sense, but guessing was not recommended on the SAT. And he wouldn't have time to read each question four damn times.

He put his head in his hands. "What have I done?"

Chance came loping back into the room. "Dude, you okay?"

"Just tired from all the studying."

"Want some Addys?"

He looked over to see Chance holding out his hand. On his palm was a little pile of orange capsules.

"They'll make you laser focused. I take them when Hannah wants oral sex."

Wes winced. "You still moving pills?"

"Selling off all my stock. I got a kid coming, man... I can't have drugs laying around." He closed his hand. "Here, take them. You gotta pass that test, dude."

True. But he also didn't want to take amphetamines that might send him back down the road to addiction.

"Come on, man, your dad's waiting for me."

Wes put out his hand. Chance dropped the smooth capsules into his palm, then hurried to the door and left.

Wes's phone rang. He glanced at the screen to see Meg's name. Since her father had caught him leaving her room, he'd avoided her, for her sake, until he could offer her a better version of himself. He sent the call to voice mail, then looked back to the Adderall.

He didn't want to take them... but he needed an advantage.

CHAPTER 18

CARLOTTA STARED up at her bedroom ceiling and sighed. She'd been plagued with bouts of insomnia since Patricia's death, but lately, it had worsened.

And tonight it was brutal.

She turned her head to glance at the clock—3:15 AM.

She groaned and sat up, then swung her legs over the edge of the bed. Her little tête-à-tête with Rainie hadn't helped matters. The woman made her feel as if she was falling down on her bridal duties, both in planning the wedding and knowing more about her groom.

The one bright spot was the hint that Jack was looking into Peter's death, although the mention of the detective dredged up more anxiety and mixed feelings. He had no business interjecting himself between her and Coop regarding the DNA samples.

She pushed to her feet and wiped at the perspiration on her neck. Maybe if she turned up the air conditioner, she could get back to sleep.

She pushed her feet into slippers, then walked out into the hallway. The door to Wes's room was ajar. She frowned and scanned the floor in the dim lighting, expecting to see his python coiled up ready to spring on her. When the coast seemed clear, she pushed open Wes's door and smiled to see he'd fallen asleep while studying.

After pulling his door closed, she consulted the thermostat. The temperature was suspiciously high, and a red blinking light told her why—the air conditioner wasn't working.

She groaned and trudged to the kitchen to get a cold drink of water. When she opened the freezer to get ice, she spotted the baggie with the condom where she'd stowed it after Jack and Coop had shot down her attempt to track down the donor.

She filled a glass with water from the tap, then drank deeply. She held the cold glass to her neck and sighed in relief. A fan would help to cool her room. She remembered seeing one in the garage, but she didn't want to go out there at this hour.

The longer she stood in the kitchen, though, the more she rationalized she could've already gone to the garage and come back with the fan and be on her way to sleep. She heaved a sigh, then backtracked to the front entrance. After disabling the alarm, she swung open the door. The thick humidity of the summer night blanketed her. Compared to the busyness of the area during the day, it was eerily still outside. She stepped out onto the stoop and looked to the left thinking this would be the only time of the day she wouldn't have to worry about running into Mrs. Winningham, their nosy neighbor.

The front of the garage was illuminated with an overhead light, so the short walk was perfectly safe. In fact, it was peaceful to walk in the moonlight when no one else was awake. When she reached the garage, she punched in the code to activate the opener, thankful for its quiet operation as the door rose.

She waited for her eyes to adjust to the low lighting, lamenting that she hadn't brought her phone. Her convertible sat in the middle of the garage. Wes's bicycle was parked nearby. She scanned shelves for the fan, but didn't see it. Surmising it had been moved during the renovations, she sighed and leaned against her car. The cool smoothness of the metal felt good under her hand. On impulse, she hopped over the door and slid into the driver's seat, then settled into the soft leather upholstery. It felt cool and cozy.

A yawn overtook her and she lay her head back, giving in to fatigue.

When she started awake, daylight streamed into the garage. She stretched high, then climbed out of the car, massaging her neck. Since Wes's bicycle was gone, she assumed he'd already gone to work and had left her sleeping. As she walked back to the stoop, she distantly registered noises of morning traffic—the neighborhood was coming alive.

"Carlotta!"

She winced, then looked up to see her neighbor standing at the fence, holding her dog Toofers. "Good morning, Mrs. Winningham."

"I wanted to say thank you." The woman smiled, and Carlotta realized for once the dog wasn't snarling.

"What for?" Carlotta asked.

"That husband of yours is so nice."

Carlotta squinted. "Coop? He's not my husband yet."

"He cut my grass." Her neighbor swept a hand to indicate her freshly cut yard.

That was odd—when did Coop have time to cut her neighbor's grass? "Oh, well, he's a really nice man."

"I know… you make such an odd couple."

At the backhanded insult, Carlotta pushed her tongue into her cheek. "Have a nice day, Mrs. Winningham."

She climbed the steps and pushed open the door. At a noise from the kitchen, she realized Wes was still home and preparing breakfast. "Wes?"

Coop appeared at the door with a smile. "No, it's me."

She smiled at the unexpected surprise. "I'm sorry—I slept in."

"I know," he said, dropping a kiss on her nose. "I thought you needed some rest. I made pancakes. Have a seat."

She sat at the table and once again thought how comfortable he seemed in her kitchen. She noticed a photo of an apple-cheeked girl of about ten stuck to the refrigerator with a magnet and wondered if it was someone Wes knew. "What a cute little girl."

"Isn't she?"

"What's her name?"

Coop gave a little laugh. "Did you hit your head? That's Lola. You named Hannah's little girl yourself."

Carlotta squinted. "Hannah has a little girl?"

Coop walked to the table and set a tall stack of pancakes in front of her. "And another on the way. At least this time your kids will grow up together."

"Hm?"

"Well, okay, you're due one month before Hannah, but it's almost the same." He bent down and placed a kiss on her very pregnant belly.

Carlotta stared in shock. "How did that happen?"

Coop laughed. "The regular way. I know we don't have much time alone between our schedules, but we seem to make it count." He looked up as three boys in stair-step ages of eight, seven, and six walked in, all neatly groomed. "Good morning, kids."

"Good morning, Dad, good morning, Mom," they chorused, then politely took seats at the table while Carlotta stared.

"Did you make your beds?" Coop asked, serving up pancakes to each child.

"Yes, sir," they chorused.

"Homework all done?"

"Yes, sir."

"Good job," Coop said. "Who's the best Mommy in the world?"

"Our mommy!" they cheered.

Coop pulled her to her feet and kissed her. "You're the best wife in the world, too. I'm so happy, Carlotta."

"Carlotta…. *Carlotta*."

She opened her eyes to see Coop leaning over her. She startled, then looked around, panicked, to get her bearings. "What? Where am I?"

"Easy," he soothed. "You must've fallen asleep out here." He opened the car door and helped her stand.

"It was hot in the house… I think the A/C is out. I came out here to get a fan, but I couldn't find it in the dark."

"You must've gotten tired and climbed in the car."

She nodded. "I had a weird dream."

"About?"

She looked up and took in his sweet, handsome face. "About us, actually."

He smiled. "Was it good?"

She bit into her lip and nodded. "It was."

"You'll have to tell me all about it."

"Why are you here? Is everything okay?"

"Everything's fine. I just got worried because you weren't answering your phone."

She saw that Wes's bike was still sitting next to her car. "Wes isn't up yet."

"He's not answering his phone either," Coop said.

"He fell asleep studying."

Coop smiled. "He wants to do well on the SAT."

She bit into her lip. "What are his chances?"

"If he gets an average score, he should be able to get into a state school."

"And if he doesn't?"

"He can study and take it again in time for admission next spring."

But she knew that kind of a delay would seem interminable to Wes, especially now that he'd told their dad he didn't want to be a partner in the golf center. It wasn't easy for him to stand up to their charismatic, accomplished father. This test represented much more than just an academic exercise—he needed a home run for his confidence.

They walked into the townhouse and Coop put on a pot of coffee. When he turned, he wet his lips. "Carlotta, the other reason I stopped by is I wanted to talk about the other day at the lab."

She put up her hands. "I was wrong, Coop. I'm sorry I put you in that position."

He looked troubled. "And I'm sorry I didn't realize that you're still so upset about Patricia's death. You shouldn't have to go through this alone, Carlotta. But obviously I've done something to make you feel like you can't share your worries with me."

She studied him, bowled over that she was going to marry this wonderful man. "It's nothing you've done, Coop. It's all on me. And besides, I've decided I'm going to put all of it behind me and accept that Patricia's death was simply an unfortunate accident."

Carlotta walked over and slid her body against his, eliciting a groan. "Let's talk about the honeymoon."

CHAPTER 19

"THAT WAS some dream," Dr. Denton said. "You seemed to have turned some kind of corner, Carlotta. You've decided to set aside your fixation on mysteries you can't solve, and you seem more excited about your own life."

"I am," Carlotta said, nodding. She'd been making herself and everyone around her crazy with her theories about how Patricia might have died. But the truth was, she might never know what had happened, and all the sleuthing in the world wasn't going to bring Patricia back. She should be focused on the life-changing event of her wedding that would affect every day of the rest of her life. "It's odd that something as inconsequential as a dream would have such an impact on my mindset."

"Not really," the doctor said. "I believe dreams are a form of self-therapy."

She squinted. "You mean I dreamed what I needed to dream?"

"Something like that. When we sleep, we co-mingle memories with imagination. That's why some dreams seem realistic, some seem fanciful, and some are a blend. Because dreams are a safe place to act out impulses, it's not uncommon to dream an alternate version of reality."

"Kind of like a rehearsal?"

He nodded. "Exactly. In dreams we can experience things without suffering the consequences, which isn't possible in real life."

"That makes sense."

He referred to his notes. "So have you shared the truth about your birth father with your fiancé?"

"Not yet," she admitted. "There's another matter I need to take care of first."

"And what is that?"

She hesitated. "I have a half-sister."

"Ah. Does she know?"

"No. And it's complicated because we're already acquainted."

His eyes widened slightly. "And do you have a good relationship?"

"No. I tried to initiate a friendship, but she wasn't interested."

"And do you think she'd feel differently if she knew you were blood related?"

"Maybe. I do."

"You said you were going to take care of it—does that mean you're going to tell her?"

"I haven't decided. Things could go sideways... a lot of people could get hurt."

He nodded. "It's wise to consider the fallout, but you can't know for sure how people will respond."

She shifted in her chair. "My family is finally getting to a good place. I don't want to be the one who blows it up."

"Do you have to make a decision right away?"

"No. But... I think she needs me. She just lost her father, and her husband is cheating on her."

"It's compassionate of you to be thinking of her in that way. But you have to be prepared for the fact that even if this woman learns you're half-sisters, she might want nothing to do with you."

Carlotta nodded, then sighed.

A tiny chime sounded, indicating they were out of time. Carlotta left the appointment feeling more torn than ever. On the way home, she stopped in a library to access a public computer and pulled up the email for the address she'd used to register her DNA.

Tracey had sent her a second email. Her heart was racing double-time when she clicked on the message.

Hello, I'm sending a second note in case you didn't receive the first one I sent. I would like to meet you and to know how we are related. Family is important to me. I hope you will respond. Tracey

Family is important to me. As she suspected, Tracey was grieving the loss of her father and the betrayal of her husband.

Carlotta sat and stared at the note until a librarian gently informed her others were waiting to use the machine. She took a deep breath, then hit Reply.

Hello... Yes, I would like for us to meet. Family is important to me, too, which is why I think we should get together in person. I also live in Atlanta. Please respond and let me know how you would like to proceed. C.

Her hand hovered over the Send button for a full minute before she pushed it.

CHAPTER 20

CARLOTTA SCANNED the whiteboard where she'd posted photos and diagrammed her theory about what might've happened the night Patricia had died. With a resolute sigh, she removed the photo of her and Patricia that had been taken at the wedding expo, then tucked it into the top drawer of her desk. She reached to take down the photo of Colleen Mason, then stopped when she heard the arrival of a vehicle. She stepped to the window and looked out, then smiled to see Coop's car.

As she walked through the hall to the front door, she noticed how much lighter she felt since deciding to focus on the wedding. The absence of a gown gnawed at her, but she trusted Jarold Jett to come through for her.

When she opened the door, Coop was chatting with Mrs. Winningham over the fence and petting her dog. Carlotta shook her head to see how easily he could charm the crotchety woman. Then he climbed the steps two at a time and met her with a kiss.

"I brought muffins."

She smiled, then waved to her neighbor. "Of course you did. Come in."

He stepped over the threshold. "It feels good in here, you must've gotten the A/C fixed."

"It was a fuse or something, but yes, thankfully, it's back on." She gestured to the kitchen. "Wes made coffee before he left. He's been living on caffeine to study."

"I've never seen anyone so determined to do well."

"You were probably like that at his age," she said, walking ahead of him.

"Maybe," he admitted. "What I meant is you've done a great job raising him."

Carlotta gave a little laugh as she removed coffee mugs from a cabinet. She filled them both, then handed one to Coop. "I can't tell you how many times I wanted to adopt him out."

"But you didn't."

"Family is important," she murmured into her coffee, then took a sip. She wondered if Tracey had read her email and if the woman had changed her mind about meeting since Carlotta had suggested an in-person introduction. Tracey might insist they trade names and vital statistics over email or phone, but Carlotta knew her only chance at forging a bond with Tracey would be to explain the situation face to face.

"You have a good family," Coop said earnestly. "You've been through a lot together."

She nodded, hoping she wasn't on the verge of doing something that would change their dynamic permanently.

When they settled at the breakfast bar, Carlotta smiled. "I could get used to having breakfast with you every morning."

He laughed. "Then it's a good thing we're getting married." He took a drink of coffee, then his expression turned serious. "Actually, I've been thinking about our conversation the other day about you living at my place. Why don't you go ahead and move in?"

She angled her head. "I thought we agreed not to sleep together until the wedding."

"I know, but it would be more convenient as the wedding gets closer to be together more," he cajoled. "Plus we could get into a routine."

"We have the rest of our lives to get into a routine." She made a rueful noise. "Besides, I don't want to leave Wes alone right now."

Coop frowned. "Are you worried he's going to lapse into old habits?"

"Maybe," she said, nodding. "I see all the signs. Wes has a way of sabotaging himself."

"You know him better than anyone." He popped the last bite of muffin into his mouth. "I need to get to the office. Don't get up—enjoy your coffee. Call me later?"

She nodded and lifted her mouth for a kiss. When he left, her mind drifted to the paperwork waiting on her desk. The commission for the Reeder job had hit her bank account, so she needed to get serious about acquiring a van for her business. And the pile of wedding RSVPs continued to accumulate.

She lifted her mug for another drink to postpone her workday for a few luxurious minutes. The sound of a vehicle in the driveway reached her and she wondered if Coop had returned. A glance out the window revealed the arrival of a delivery truck. Between her own supplies and the supplies Valerie had ordered for the StyleMe Hangers, delivery vehicles were coming and going all the time—something else for Mrs. Winningham to complain about.

But the refrigerator-sized box the driver unloaded was perplexing. "Whatever it is," he called up to her, "it's big, but not very heavy." The side of the box read, 'fabric contents, do not open with sharp tool.'

She gasped—her dress!

When they determined the box wouldn't fit through the front door, Carlotta directed him to bring it to the rear of the house to the sliding glass doors leading from her office to the back deck. In order to make room for the enormous box, she moved the whiteboard to a closet and pushed a chair to the wall. After the enormous box was parked, she confirmed the shipper was Jett Designs, then signed for it and thanked the driver.

She hurried to locate a pair of blunt shears, then worked to loosen the seals on the box. Throughout her heart thudded nervously—what if she didn't like it? And despite sending careful measurements, what if it didn't fit? With only two weeks left before the wedding, she'd be forced to buy something off the rack.

Or worse—at a bridal discount warehouse.

She set aside the depressing thought and opened the box to reveal mounds of tissue paper around a white bell-shaped garment bag. Fastened to the front was a small envelope with "Carlotta" written on it in large, flourishing handwriting. She hung the bag on a rack, then opened the envelope and pulled out a card.

My dear Carlotta, I'm enclosing a special dress for your special day. I hope you and your detective cowboy will be very happy. With gratitude, Jarold Jett

Carlotta pushed her tongue into her cheek. Jarold had met Jack during the wedding expo and commented on their chemistry… apparently the man assumed *they* were tying the knot.

She pushed the gross misunderstanding from her mind and turned back to the dress. Her hands shook as she unzipped the garment bag and pulled it away.

Wonder filled her chest.

The strapless gown was a confection of white silk covered with a layer of the finest white tulle. The deep vee neckline was shaped by a swath of tulle that wrapped under one breast and down to cinch the waist. After accentuating the hips, the dress narrowed at the knees, hugging every curve.

But the main feature of the gown was the froth of curlicue fabric that began at the knee and ballooned out before falling gracefully to the floor, creating a six-foot train in the back. The veil was a simple cloud of tulle, short to offset the fullness of the train.

Carlotta covered her mouth with her hands, enchanted. It was a magical dress, more special than she could've hoped for.

A sign that her wedding day would be perfect.

CHAPTER 21

"HAVE YOU ever thought about how you'll die?"

Wes looked up from his study guide to stare at Kendall Abrams, his creepy coworker at the morgue. The guy was odd-looking and odd-acting, but Coop had said he couldn't be choosy about his deniers because college-age kids weren't lining up to intern at the county morgue like they were lining up to work at Apple.

The fact that Kendall's uncle was a former Medical Examiner at the morgue and a bona fide serial killer gave him a certain amount of street cred in the autopsy room, and he was decent at his job. But at the moment, he was like an icepick to the brain.

"Nope." Wes took a swig of an energy drink and looked back to his book.

"I think I'll burn up in a fire."

"Cool."

"Or be shot in a mugging."

Wes sighed. "You're dwelling again. Change the channel."

"Suffocating in the cargo compartment of a plane wouldn't be so bad."

"Dude, you're killing *me* right now. Stop talking so I can study."

"I got something to help with that," Kendall said.

"If it's Adderall, I already got some." But they were still in his pocket, messing with his already short attention-span. He had only three more days to cram and at this rate, he'd have to take the Addys to stop thinking about the Addys.

"Nah, something else, it's in my locker. I'll be back, man."

Wes shook his head. Knowing Kendall it was probably a piece of good-luck taxidermy, like a shriveled rabbit's head.

His phone buzzed and he knew without looking it was Meg again—something else to mess with his concentration. He missed her so much his skin hurt. But he was determined to be a boyfriend she could be proud of and someone her father would allow to walk through the front door.

He turned back to the study book and completed a sample test, but when he checked his answers in the back, he was demoralized. He was going to humiliate himself.

Kendall came back in the room and slapped a manilla envelope on the table.

"What's that?" Wes asked.

"It's the SAT test."

He pointed at his study book. "Thanks, man, but I got all kinds of sample tests."

"It's not a sample test, it's *the* test, with answers."

Wes narrowed his eyes. "How's that possible?"

Kendall smiled. "I know people."

Wes shook his head. "No, man, I can't cheat."

"Sure you can," Kendall said. "Lots of people do. So if you don't, you look like a dumbass, and someone who cheated will get your spot this fall." He lifted his hands. "What does it matter? You just gotta get in, right? Then you play it straight and do the classwork."

When he put it that way... "How much?"

"No charge," Kendall said, clapping him on the shoulder. "You're my best friend."

While he digested that sad little morsel, Kendall jerked his thumb toward the door. "Gotta go. They just brought in an exhumed body to be re-autopsied, and I want a front row seat."

Wes let the envelope lie there until Kendall walked away. It wasn't lost on him that he'd just been handed the key to the club he was desperate to join. He picked up the envelope and hefted it in his hands. It even felt substantial... like the information it contained was valuable.

He looked over his shoulder, then ran his finger under the flap to partially break the seal.

Footsteps sounded behind him. "Hey, Wes," Coop said.

Wes shoved the envelope under his arm and turned. "Hey."

"Sorry to interrupt your lunch."

"I was using my lunch break to study."

Coop smiled. "Good for you. This is good practice for med school."

The envelope felt lumpy and conspicuous. "If you say so."

"I just wanted to make sure you're available for the bachelor party Jack is putting together at Moody's. June says you can come, but you can't drink. Sorry."

"That's okay," Wes said, starting to sweat.

Coop grinned. "I won't be drinking either, so you can keep me company."

"Yeah, sure."

"Invite your buddy Chance if you want to."

He swallowed past a suddenly-dry throat. "Okay, will do."

"And, um, just so you know, I didn't invite Kendall."

Wes nodded. "Good call."

"I'll let you get back to studying," Coop said. "You're going to do great on the test, I'm sure of it."

"Thanks, man."

When Coop walked away, Wes exhaled and picked up the envelope. The contents were calling to him, just like the Adderall in his pocket.

He considered giving the test back to Kendall, but he suspected Kendall wouldn't take it... and knowing it was in the guy's locker would be too tempting.

Using all of his restraint, he picked up his phone and connected a call.

"Wes... how are you, Little Man?"

"Hi, Mouse. I'm good. Studying for the SAT exam with the book you gave me."

"No kidding? That's great."

"I need another favor, Mouse."

"Name it."

"I don't trust myself. I need to hand off something to get it out of reach."

"Okay. No problem. Where are you?"

"I'm working at the county morgue today.'"

"I'm near there, give me fifteen minutes?"

Wes exhaled. "I'll be in the parking lot." He ended the call, then stuck the envelope inside his study book and headed toward the exit. He stuck his hand in his pocket to finger the Addys he still hadn't taken—if he ditched the test, he'd have to rely on old-fashioned studying, so didn't he deserve to give himself an edge?

He changed his mind five times on the way out to the parking lot. He could hand Mouse the Addys and keep the test... or hand him the test and keep the Addys.

When the familiar black Town Car pulled into view, he still hadn't decided what to do.

The driver's side window buzzed down and Mouse's big ugly mug came into view. "Hiya, Wes."

Wes grinned. "Good to see you, Mouse."

"Good to see you. You look like a doctor already."

Wes looked down at his white lab coat. "I'm just a flunky, but I like the job."

"When do you take the SAT exam?"

"In three days."

"Will you be ready?"

Wes chewed on his lip. Would he? If he bombed the test, he would disappoint so many people.

He considered the big man who'd gone out of his way to save his skinny ass more than once, and who'd believed in him when nobody else did. He couldn't let Mouse down, and that meant doing his best and taking his lumps.

"I'll be ready," he said. He slid the envelope out of the book and handed it to Mouse through the window.

"Want me to keep it or get rid of it?"

"Get rid of it."

"Will do. Good luck on your test, Little Man. Let me know how it goes."

In his pocket, he was stroking the Addy capsules. "Okay."

The window began to buzz up.

"Wait," Wes said.

Mouse arched an eyebrow.

Wes pulled his hand out of his pocket and held it out. Mouse stuck a meaty paw out the window and Wes dropped the capsules into his big hand. "Get rid of those, too."

Mouse nodded. "Got it. Take care, Wes."

The window buzzed up and the Town Car circled around to the exit, then disappeared from view.

Wes slogged back to the lobby, feeling depressed. Doing the right thing sucked sometimes.

"There he is… hey, Wes."

He lifted his head and blinked in surprise to see Coop… talking to Meg. She was luminous in a short lavender romper and sandals, her hair pulled back in a high ponytail.

His heart was beating out of his scrawny chest. "What are you doing here?"

"Checking to see if you were dead," she said. "Since you won't answer the phone."

"I'm not dead… I've been busy."

"Coop just told me—you're taking the SAT?" Her face lit up.

"Yeah," he said, holding up his study book. "In three days… but I don't know how well I'll do."

She crossed her arms. "You'll do great, because I aced it and I'll help you study."

His mood bounced. "You will?"

"Of course."

"Wes," Coop said, "why don't you take the rest of the day off to study? I'll make sure you get credit for the hours."

He grinned. "Thanks, Coop."

Meg gestured to his book. "So let's get started."

"Won't your dad be upset if he finds out you're with me?"

"Probably," she admitted. "I'll just tell him I'm hanging out with Mark."

Wes gritted his teeth, then nodded, hoping someday she wouldn't have to hide him from her parents.

CHAPTER 22

CARLOTTA SORTED the mail, stacking more wedding RSVPs in a pile and separating out her business mail.

One small envelope was of nice quality stationery with the initials DR beautifully printed on the flap. Inside was a personal thank you note from Delinda Reeder for Carlotta's assistance with her wardrobe. A thoughtful gesture, she noted, and she'd enjoyed getting to know the woman. When she set aside the envelope she realized something else was inside. She pulled out a folded sheet of paper—a copy of the non-disclosure agreement she'd signed.

She pushed her tongue into her cheek. A courtesy, or a subtle reminder?

Her phone rang and she smiled to see Coop's name on the screen. She connected the call. "Hello, you."

"Hi there. Did I call at a bad time?"

"No, I'm doing paperwork. I'm going to try to get to the wedding RSVPs today. We have to give the hotel a final number in a few days."

"The countdown begins," he said lightly. "I know you feel relieved to have your dress."

"Oh, yes. I know it seems silly to men, but it's important to most women that they feel like everything is just right on their wedding day."

"I get it," he said. "I want it to be the happiest day of your life."

"It will be," she sang. "What are you up to?"

He made a rueful noise. "I called to give you an update. You were right—Colleen Mason didn't commit suicide."

She blinked at the unexpected news. "How do you know?"

"The D.A. and her family quietly had her body exhumed for another autopsy. There were drugs in her system, but not enough to cause the respiratory failure that killed her. Her cause of death has been reclassified as inconclusive."

Her pulse skipped a beat. "Will there be an investigation?"

"It looks like it. The news hasn't been released to the media yet, but I just wanted to say... good call."

Her mind raced to process the information. The news of an alleged mistress dying under suspicious circumstances could mean more trouble for the Reeder family and the campaign. And would it lead to Patricia's case being reopened? "Thank you, Coop, for believing me and talking to the D.A."

Silence sounded. "I didn't talk to the D.A.—Jack did."

Her eyes widened. "Jack?"

"You must've said something to make him rethink the evidence."

Would wonders never cease. "So what happens now?"

"That's up to Jack and the D.A. My office will stand by to assist as needed."

At the sound of a vehicle arriving in the driveway, Carlotta pushed aside the curtain to see Jack climbing out of his dark sedan.

"Jack just pulled up," she said. "I should go."

"Call me later?"

"Of course," she murmured, then ended the call.

She sprinted to the front door and flung it open. Jack was walking up the steps, wincing at the sharp barks and snarling coming from Toofers on the other side of the fence.

"You parked on the grass," Mrs. Winningham yelled to Jack, gesturing to his car. "We like to keep our yards looking nice around here."

"I won't be long," Jack called back, then rolled his eyes at Carlotta.

She bit back a smile, then affected innocence. "Jack... what brings you around?"

He gave her a flat smile. "Cut the crap, Carlotta. I'm sure you've talked to Coop—he probably couldn't wait to call his girlfriend and tell her she was right."

She stepped back to allow him to walk inside. "Why does it irritate you when I'm right, Jack?"

"Because it only encourages you to meddle more where you don't belong."

She crossed her arms. "Is this the part where you ask me to hand over all the evidence I've been accumulating?"

He frowned. "Don't gloat. Just show me what you've got."

She led him back to her office where she dragged the whiteboard from the closet and reviewed her theory of the switched makeup cases and the players involved. Jack asked a few questions, but mostly listened.

Carlotta picked up her phone. "I'm texting you the photos I took of Patricia's hotel room." Jack's phone buzzed and he nodded that he'd received them.

She pulled a plastic bag from a drawer that held a phone. "Here's Patricia's phone that was found by the hotel dumpster. And—" She dragged two big cardboard boxes from a closet. "Here are all the items that were removed from Patricia's hotel room."

"And the makeup case is in there?"

She nodded. "I wore gloves when I examined it. Hopefully Colleen Mason's fingerprints are on it."

Jack didn't comment, but she knew he was thinking that was a longshot considering who knew how many people had handled it at the death scene and when packing it up. "Anything else?"

"Do you want the condom and the cigarette?"

"No." Jack's mouth tightened. "But... don't get rid of them."

She leaned against her desk. "Does this mean Patricia's case will be reopened?"

"I can't make any promises," Jack said, "but I'm going to go over everything carefully and see where it leads."

She bit into her lip. "Thank you, Jack."

He sighed. "I should know by now that you have good instincts for trouble."

She scoffed. "Is that a compliment?"

"Maybe," he said with a little smile. His expression changed to pensive. "You asked me why I get irritated when you're right about things like this. It's because you remind me of someone I used to know."

She squinted. "Who?"

He wet his lips, then shook his head. "It doesn't matter." He glanced around the room and pursed his mouth. "Your office is looking nice."

"Thanks. Business is good, thankfully."

His attention snagged on the oversized white garment bag hanging from a rack. "Hey, you found a wedding dress."

"Actually, I took your advice and contacted Jarold Jett, and he sent me the perfect dress."

"Nice."

"Want to hear something funny? He thought you and I were getting married."

His dark eyebrows shot up. "Yeah... that's funny, alright. Imagine me and you, married."

Their gazes locked, and she experienced a montage of snippets of their rollercoaster relationship—the arguing, the sex, the hurt, the friendship. She wondered if he was having his own walk down memory lane. When the silence became awkward, she pushed away from her desk. "Do you need a hand getting these things to the car?"

Jack blinked, then came back from wherever he'd been. "Sure."

CHAPTER 23

"AND... TIME," the test administrator said, holding up a stopwatch. "Pencils down. Please close your test booklet and answer sheet, and place them back in the labeled envelope. Seal the envelope and return it to me before you leave. You will receive your scores in two to three weeks."

Wes put down his pencil, too mentally exhausted to feel anything other than relief the exam was behind him. He followed the instructions and glanced around at the test takers who were left—about twenty-five percent of the original group. Were they the dummies? Time would tell.

He stood and joined the line, waiting his turn to drop his test. As luck would have it, the test administrator was one of Chance's former professors.

When Wes held out his envelope, the guy narrowed his eyes. "Weren't you in my Economics class last term?"

Wes shook his head. "Wrong guy. I'm trying to get into college."

"Right." The man took his envelope, the matter forgotten.

When he left the building, he lifted his face to the sunshine and exhaled. He had no idea how he'd done on the test—most of the questions were various degrees of impossible, and the ones that seemed easy made him second-guess himself. Regardless, it was done. Now he could only wait.

And hope.

As he unlocked his bicycle, he checked his watch. He didn't have to report to the morgue for another two hours. He considered going back to the townhouse to take a nap, but he felt too antsy to sleep. He was too far away from the golf center to make the trip worthwhile. He wanted to see Meg, but her father...

Wes stopped and ground his jaw, then jumped on his bike and started peddling.

On the way to the Vincent house, he practiced his boyfriend speech. But when the door opened and Dr. Vincent stood there, staring at him with unveiled loathing, his mind blanked.

Dr. Vincent rolled his eyes. "Did you want something?"

Wes straightened. "I'd like to see Meg."

"What part of 'I don't want you to see my daughter' do you not understand?"

Wes took a deep, shaky breath. "I understand. But here's the thing—I love Meg... and she loves me. You don't have to like me now, but I'm going to do everything I can to prove to you that I deserve to be with your daughter." He stabbed at his glasses. "Sir."

Harold Vincent studied him and Wes imagined all the unflattering things the man saw in him—a skinny, broke, uneducated, uncouth delinquent with a questionable future. He was probably trying to decide whether to slam the door, call the police, or pull out one of his hunting rifles.

"In that case," Dr. Vincent said with the whisper of a smile on his face, "you'd better come in."

The man stepped back and after a few seconds of stupefied shock, Wes walked through the front door.

CHAPTER 24

HELLO, CAN you meet tomorrow at the Starbucks at the Lenox Mall at 10AM? I'm twenty-nine years old, and I have short, dark hair. How will I know you? Tracey

Carlotta scanned the email on her new tablet. Her heart lodged in her throat. If she met with Tracey, there would be no going back, no unknowing of the truth... and she had no inkling for how the woman would react to the news.

She inhaled deeply, hoping for clarity. It would be easier to let sleeping dogs lie. Maybe in time she could earn Tracey's friendship and break the news to her when things were less contentious. Although without knowledge of a blood-bond, she doubted Tracey would ever give her the time of day, especially when Tracey blamed her for Walt's incarceration.

On its own volition, her finger hit the Reply button. Carlotta typed a response, telling herself she could delete it at the end.

Hello, Yes, I can meet you then. I will wear a red scarf. C.

Her finger hovered over the Send button. She would sleep on it, and if she woke up tomorrow and realized meeting Tracey was a bad idea, she'd cancel. She clicked the button, then puffed out her cheeks in a long exhale.

At the sound of Coop's car pulling in, she jumped up and grabbed her purse. She hurried to the door and locked it behind her, then jogged down the steps.

"Carlotta," Mrs. Winningham said from the fence. "Are you running a business out of your home? If you are, that's not good for the neighborhood and our home values."

Carlotta stopped and extended an envelope over the fence.

"What's this?" the woman asked.

"An invitation to my wedding," Carlotta said.

The woman's lips parted as she took the envelope. "You're inviting me to your wedding?"

"Of course. I hope you can attend."

"I... will have to buy a new dress."

"It's always nice to have an occasion to buy a new dress."

The woman actually smiled. "Th-Thank you, Carlotta."

"You're welcome. Bye, Mrs. Winningham."

She walked to Coop's restored corvette and climbed in. "Hello, you."

He leaned in for a kiss. "Hello, you. Are you ready to buy our wedding rings?"

"Absolutely."

He put the car in gear and turned around. "Are you on a schedule?"

"Not today. I'm all yours."

"I hope so."

She turned her head. "Hm?"

"I hope you're all mine today because I have something planned for later."

"Ooh, I'm intrigued."

He gave her a playful smile. "Good."

They drove to the jewelry store where he'd purchased her engagement ring. When the saleswoman pulled trays of matching wedding bands from a glass case, Carlotta was unprepared for the emotional impact—the pairs of rings underlined the commitment they were making to each other.

"Did you have something in mind?" the woman asked.

Coop looked to her, but she shook her head, suddenly and unexplainably nervous.

"Gold, silver, titanium?" the woman prompted.

"Um, gold?" Coop suggested.

Carlotta nodded.

"Etched or plain?" the clerk asked.

"I think the etched ones are nice," Coop said.

"Yes," she murmured.

"How about these?" Coop pointed to a pair with a script design.

When she didn't respond, he squeezed her hand.

"Carlotta, are you with us?"

She gave herself a mental shake. "Yes. I love those—they're gorgeous."

The woman removed the rings and handed one to each of them. Carlotta slid the band onto her finger and stared. The engagement ring had represented a promise, but the wedding ring...

"Makes if feel real, doesn't it?" Coop asked softly, holding his beringed hand up to hers.

She smiled. "Yes. It'll take some getting used to."

"That's what most married people say... about everything." He angled his head. "What do you think, should we take these?"

She nodded. "Yes, let's take these."

"That was easy," the saleswoman said. "Most couples aren't so agreeable." She smiled. "I'll box these up for you."

Coop pulled her close and kissed her temple. "Are you up for a drive?"

"That sounds wonderful," she said, thinking the open air might help to clear her mind. She was letting the thought of meeting Tracey tomorrow distract her, and it wasn't fair to Coop.

With the boxed rings tucked away in the trunk, Coop steered the Corvette to a pretty area of town that bordered the sprawling, thriving Piedmont Park. "I love this area," Carlotta said, taking in the beautiful old homes and the brick sidewalks.

"They don't build homes like this anymore," Coop agreed. "Why don't we park the car and walk? There's an ice cream place on the next block."

"I'd like that."

He guided the car into an empty spot on the street, then walked around to open her door. When she stepped out, he clasped her hand. They strolled along the sidewalk, nodding to people they passed and lifting their hands when residents waved from their porches.

"What do you think about that house?" Coop asked, stopping in front of a Craftsman style bungalow.

The gray gabled home sat on a lush blanket of green grass. A stone walkway led from the sidewalk to the deep porch framed with white balustrade and balusters. Two of the front windows had stained glass inserts, and the front door was a welcoming blue-green.

"It's perfect," she murmured, and meant it.

The door opened and a man stepped out. Coop waved and the man waved back. "Let's go take a look."

Carlotta gave a little laugh. "We can't ask that man to give us a tour of his home."

"He's a real estate agent," Coop said. "The house just came on the market, and I got a preview. What would you think about living here?"

She couldn't hold back a smile. "I would love it."

He smiled and pulled her toward the door. Up close the exterior of the house was even more appealing, the porch more inviting. But the outside was nothing compared to the inside—original wood floors, built-in cabinetry, and two fireplaces. The kitchen had been recently updated but retained much of the authentic charm. The three bedrooms were roomy and the backyard was picturesque. And the rooms were steeped in lived-in, loved-in coziness.

"What do you think?" Coop asked. "Should we buy it?"

It was clear he'd already fallen in love with the house. And why not? It was a home where happy people lived.

Buoyed by his enthusiasm, Carlotta smiled wide. "Let's do it."

CHAPTER 25

CARLOTTA STARED at the red scarf, breathing in and out. She'd bought it on impulse when she was shopping for Delinda Reeder. Only later did she realize the tiny pattern on the scarf was two hands connected with a pinky swear, and she'd wondered if she'd been subliminally attracted to it because of the inherently sisterly symbol.

She'd arrived at the mall early, but still hadn't decided if she would go in to meet Tracey.

Was this a selfish exercise in an effort to resolve the fact that she'd never be close to her biological father?

Or was it selfish if she didn't tell Tracey she had a half-sibling?

She told herself she would know what to do when she saw Tracey's face.

After stowing the scarf in her purse, she climbed out of the Miata and headed into the mall, more nervous than she'd ever been in her life. The mall was busy today, which was always nice to see. As she moved through the wide halls, distantly registering the background music wafting through the upscale space, she mused over how much of her life had taken place in and around this complex. She'd spent her entire adult life working retail. She'd met Hannah when her friend was working at a café in the mall. And now once again what might be a pivotal moment in her life was unfolding in what was basically a public space.

Her steps slowed as she approached the Starbucks. In the adjacent seating area, Tracey Tully Lowenstein occupied a table, anxiously glancing around over the top of her lidded cup.

Carlotta stopped and studied the woman, once again thinking how pretty she was when she wasn't in mean-girl mode—in the unguarded state Tracey looked downright approachable. *This* woman she could like, *this* woman she could be friends with. While she stood, wavering, the decision was made for her when Tracey spotted her.

Instantly, Tracey looked away and pretended not to see her. She could walk away now and not only would Tracey not be the wiser, but she'd be relieved.

Carlotta took a deep breath and walked up to the table. "Hi, Tracey."

Tracey looked up and gave her a half-smile. "Hi, Carlotta. Are you back working at the mall? I thought you quit Neiman's."

"I did, but now that I'm building a personal shopping business, I'm back here often." She smiled. "Plus I have to get my own retail fix."

Tracey drank from her cup and looked around.

"Do you mind if I join you?" Carlotta asked, taking the opposite seat.

"Actually," Tracey said, "I'm meeting someone."

Carlotta hesitated, then reached into her purse and removed the scarf with a shaking hand. She lifted it around her shoulders, then met Tracey's gaze. "I know... I'm the person you're meeting."

Emotions flitted over Tracey's face, ending in confusion. "What is this, some kind of joke? I'm supposed to be meeting someone I'm related to."

Carlotta nodded. "It's me, Tracey... I'm the person whose DNA matched up to your family tree."

The woman shook her head in disbelief. *"How?"*

"We're related," Carlotta said, easing toward the truth.

"How are we related?"

She counted to three... then to five... then to ten. "We're half-sisters."

Tracey's eyes went wide. "That's impossible... that would mean..."

Carlotta watched as the implication began to dawn. "Randolph isn't my biological father," she said softly.

Tracey leaned back, away from her. "Are you saying that *my* father..."

"Is my father," Carlotta confirmed.

Tracey's chair screeched back. "I'm not listening to this nonsense. I don't know what game you're playing, Carlotta, but it's not funny."

"No, it isn't," Carlotta said. "I'm not playing any game... in fact, I had to think long and hard before replying to you, and before coming here. At least let me explain."

Tracey didn't soften, but she didn't leave.

"My mother and your father were involved when they were single. After they broke up, my mother met Randolph, then learned she was pregnant. I grew up thinking Randolph was my father. It was only recently that I learned he isn't my biological parent... but even my mother doesn't know that I know it's... Walt."

Tracey's eyes filled with tears. "This can't be true."

"I know this must come as a shock."

She put her hand to her mouth and gulped air. "Does he know?"

"Walt? I don't believe so. Valerie never told him. And to my knowledge, Randolph doesn't know either. He and Walt were good friends when they worked together."

"So the only people who know..."

"Are Valerie, me... and now you. I know you have a brother."

She nodded. "Michael is adopted, but we're very close. I don't see any reason to tell him... or my mother." She broke off on a sob.

"Of course." Carlotta reached forward to touch Tracey's hand, but she yanked away.

"*Don't.* You're the reason my father is in jail, and now you have the nerve to tell me this? Is this why you hunted him down, to get revenge?"

Carlotta shook her head. "I didn't know the truth until after Walt was arrested." She pressed her lips together to let the woman take a beat. "And the reason Walt's in jail is because of the crimes he committed. It was wrong of him to ask you to protect him."

Tracey's mouth tightened in defiance, but Carlotta suspected Michael—and possibly Tracey's mother—had told her the same thing. Her eyes welled over. "My life... is falling apart. My dad is in jail... Freddy and I are getting a divorce... and now..." She choked.

"I didn't mean to pile on," Carlotta said. "I decided to come today because... I thought you might need someone."

"I don't need your pity," Tracey bit out.

"I'm not offering you pity, Tracey. I'm offering to be your friend."

She pushed to her feet. "I can't be here—I have to go."

Carlotta stood. "Please... take this." She removed the red scarf from her shoulders and tucked it into the front pocket of Tracey's jacket. "If you decide you don't want to talk to me again, I will understand."

Tracey glared back through her tears, but the fact that she didn't throw the gift to the ground was a small victory.

CHAPTER 26

"OUR OFFER was formally accepted," Coop said. "We bought a home!"

Carlotta squealed into the phone. "I can't believe we're going to live in that beautiful house. It's a good thing I completed our gift registry yesterday—we're going to need so many things."

"What else is on our to-do list?"

"Finalize our London flights and hotel."

"I'll do that. What about giving an RSVP count to the Georgian?"

"I'll do that," she said. "The only thing left is parties and the rehearsal."

"And then we'll be married," Coop said.

"Yes," she said, unable to hold back her smile. "We'll be married."

"I have to get back to work. Call me later?"

"Of course," she said. She ended the call and gave another little squeal.

Perfect wedding.

Perfect husband.

Perfect house.

She reached for the pile of RSVPs and counted them one last time. On impulse, after she'd met with Tracey, she'd sent her a wedding invitation and invited her to the bachelorette party at Moody's. The woman probably wouldn't attend—indeed, she might not ever talk to her again—but Carlotta wanted to extend an olive branch. She looked at the final tally of RSVPs, then added one—just in case.

At the sound of a car pulling into the driveway, she glanced out the window to see Jack's sedan. Anticipation pinged through her chest—maybe he had news about Patricia's case. When she opened the door, she could tell from his stiff body language he was there on business.

"Is this a bad time?"

"No. Come in, Jack."

He stepped over the threshold and she shut the door behind him. "Want some coffee?"

He hesitated. "Got something stronger? It's been a long week."

"I think there's some brandy in the cabinet."

"That'll do."

"Have a seat, I'll get some glasses."

In the kitchen, she found two snifters, then poured an inch of brandy into each one. When she came back to the living room, he was sitting in one of the club chairs. She handed him a glass, then sat on the couch. She waited until he'd taken a drink before asking, "Do you have news?"

He nodded. "I wanted to tell you in person that Walt Tully has been charged with planning Peter's murder."

She gasped as pain sliced through her chest. "When?" she managed to get out. "How?"

"I've been working that angle for a while," Jack said, "but to be honest, I was getting nowhere. No inmates would come forward, and Walt's daughter clammed up even though the D.A. offered to drop the aiding and abetting charge if she shared what she knew." He lifted his upturned hand. "Then yesterday the daughter had a change of heart, admitted she overheard Walt on a phone call talking about staging an incident in the jail, and she turned over a burner phone he used when he was hiding out."

Carlotta brought her fist to her mouth. She knew what it must have cost Tracey to give up Walt. Hopefully she'd done it out of decency and not because she was lashing out over the news Carlotta had shared.

"I'm sorry," he said. "I know this dredges up Peter's death again... and it must be terrible to know his death was so... transactional."

She nodded, wiping at her eyes. She took a drink of the brandy, welcoming the burn of the alcohol as it slid down her tight throat.

Jack took a drink from his glass. "I lost someone, too."

Confused, she glanced at Jack to find him staring off into the distance.

"It was a long time ago," he continued. "A woman I was seeing... we were young, I had just joined the force in Birmingham." He looked into the glass, swirled the amber liquid. "She was murdered. Someone broke into her apartment and cut her throat, for no apparent reason. The case was never solved, but I always thought it was someone I'd arrested trying to get back at me."

Carlotta was riveted, both by the horrific story, and that Jack was sharing it. "How awful for you, Jack. What was her name?"

He tipped up the glass for a drink. "Serena."

The name of his boat, she realized with a start.

He sighed. "I left Birmingham and came to Atlanta to start over, but... it was always there." He looked up. "The other day when I said you reminded me of someone, it was her." He smiled suddenly. "She was a spitfire, and independent as hell. And God, so beautiful."

At the emotion in his voice, her heart cracked for him.

"Her dying broke me. It's why I pour myself into the job, I guess." He wet his lips. "It's why I've never been able to tell you... what you wanted to hear."

Her lips parted. "Jack—"

"It's good that you're marrying Coop," he cut in, then killed the rest of the drink. "I've done things that hurt you... the Liz situation." He shook his head. "And I should've told you when I first realized that Randolph isn't your biological father. Instead I watched it coming at you like a slow-moving train."

She cupped her glass tightly. "Randolph *is* my real dad." She hesitated. "I just found out my biological father killed Peter."

Jack stopped, then his eyes widened in realization. He made a mournful sound, then reached over to clasp her hand. "I'm sorry... about so many things."

Carlotta squeezed his fingers. "So am I."

He released her hand abruptly, then set down the glass and pushed to his feet. "I should go. By the way... I might be starting to believe your theory about the makeup case swap."

She inhaled sharply. "You are?"

"I asked the hotel for the security footage the night Patricia died, and they're working on it." He pulled on his chin. "Now if you can figure out how Colleen Mason was murdered, I'll give you a prize."

The phone at his belt buzzed. He glanced at the screen. "Gotta go." He smiled. "I guess I'll see you in a few days at the wedding rehearsal."

She pushed to her feet, but he was already out the door. It closed behind him with a bang.

Carlotta lifted her glass and downed the rest of the brandy.

CHAPTER 27

CARLOTTA THREADED her way across the cemetery to stop at a granite headstone. *Peter Ashford, Beloved Son and Friend*

She lay a bouquet of yellow lilies on his grave, now thick with green grass. Disbelief still rocked her that he could be gone... knowing how and why he'd died only made it seem more impossible... and useless. He had been such a beautiful man, with so much to live for.

She swallowed past a tight throat. "Hi, Peter. It's Carly." Her voice caught when she realized no one would ever call her by that pet name again.

"So much has happened, I don't know where to start. Wes is growing up, hoping to get into college soon. You were always so good to him. My family is doing well considering what we've been through. I left my job and started a business." She smiled. "I think you'd be proud of me." She wiped at her eyes.

"I'm getting married." A little laugh escaped her. "Yes, finally. I feel like it's time to settle down and maybe start my own family one day."

Her eyes welled and spilled over. "But I miss you, Peter. I miss knowing that you're around, and I'm so sad we won't be friends when we're old. I will always think of you with love."

She kissed her fingers, then touched them to his headstone. It was warm from the sun.

CHAPTER 28

"DUDE," CHANCE said. "No offense, but this is the most boring bachelor party I've ever been to. Where are the strippers?"

Wes took another drink of his Red Bull, and scanned the crew of guys gathered at Moody's Cigar bar lounge—Coop, Randolph, Jack, and a handful of Coop's friends and coworkers, all sitting around drinking brown whiskey and smoking stogies. "This is a mature bachelor party. These guys have all been castrated by women, or by life." And he got it—he'd gladly hand his balls over to Meg if she asked.

"I guess so," Chance said. "Come to think of it, I can't remember the last time I saw another woman naked other than Hannah, and that's okay."

"You're growing up," Wes confirmed. "Have you and Dad signed the paperwork on the golf center?"

Chance lit up. "Our attorneys are meeting this week. My dad is so glad I've found something to do with my trust fund."

"So is my dad," Wes said wryly.

"We decided to keep the name Wren & Son, if that's okay with you."

"No problem." In time he hoped Randolph and Chance would be as close as father and son—Chance needed a mentor, and Randolph needed someone he could mold. It was a good deal for all concerned, him included.

"I'm going to get a cigar," Chance said. "Want one?"

"Sure," Wes said. He hadn't smoked cigarettes for a while, but it couldn't be much different.

After Chance left, Wes walked over to Jack. "Nice party."

Jack quirked a smile. "Are you and your buddy bored?"

"He *was* complaining about the lack of strippers."

"Coop's not the stripper kind of guy," Jack said dryly. "Besides, I've seen more than one wedding derailed because the groom did something stupid at his bachelor party."

Wes pursed his mouth. "And you wouldn't want the wedding to be derailed, would you, Jack?"

Jack shifted and drank from his glass of whiskey. "No, I would not." His mouth lifted in a half-smile. "Tell your buddy a June-approved burlesque dancer is stopping by, strictly PG13 stuff, but it checks the box. Hey, how's your girlfriend?"

Wes tried not to smile, but he couldn't help it. "She's good... *we're* good, I think. I took your advice about making peace with her dad, and it worked."

Jack nodded. "Good."

Randolph walked up, holding a glass in one hand, a cigar in the other. "Can I join you two?"

"Sure," Jack said easily. "We were just talking about Wes's girlfriend Meg. He said she's doing well after her ordeal."

"She was lucky," Randolph agreed.

"Lucky," Jack said, "that an American with special op skills was there to rescue her."

Wes froze.

Randolph took a draw on his cigar. "Oh?"

"Yeah," Jack said. "Turns out the name Meg overheard and gave to the Irish police—Bieth—translates to Birch."

Wes sucked in a sharp breath.

Randolph pursed his mouth. "Is that so?"

"Hell of a coincidence, wouldn't you say?" Jack asked.

"Yeah," Randolph said, then waited.

And Wes waited.

"But what a can of worms," Jack said. "And I don't have time for that kind of paperwork." He lifted his glass to Randolph. "Cheers."

Randolph smiled and clinked his glass to Jack's "Cheers."

Wes exhaled.

Cabaret music blasted into the room. He turned to see a curvy blonde in pin-up makeup wearing a fur-trimmed cape and feathery headdress twirl into the room. She strutted over to Coop and began to dance to the cheers of the men in the lounge.

Wes clapped and whistled, but his gaze went to Jack who was smiling and leaning into Randolph as they talked. He realized Jack wanted to get along with Randolph, for Carlotta's sake. It gave him a different perception of the man. He was impressed.

And worried.

CHAPTER 29

"I WISH you'd let me invite a stripper," Hannah groused, glancing around the group of women gathered in the upper lounge at Moody's. Rainie was laughing with June, who'd taken the night off. Lindy had stopped by and to Carlotta's surprise, was smoking a stogie with Valerie—another surprise. "Chance said they at least had a burlesque dance at their party last night."

Carlotta shook her head. "The palm reader is a nice touch." She nodded to where the berobed woman was consulting with Quentin on a corner couch. "Everyone seems to be enjoying it. The last thing I need is an over-muscled sweaty guy grinding on me."

Hannah frowned. "I meant for *me*. I can't drink, I can't smoke. And I haven't seen any guy naked except Chance for way too long."

She laughed. "How's that situation, by the way?"

"Not bad, actually. I finally bit the bullet and told my folks Chance and I are pregnant, then sneaked in the fact that we're also married."

Carlotta smiled. "They must be happy about the baby."

"They are... and since Chance is going into business with your dad, he now looks semi-impressive. I told him he could move in with me."

"Wow, that's a big step, good for you. Have you thought about names for the baby yet?"

"If it's a boy, I'll have to name him after my dad to make up for the gene pool I'm introducing into ours. If it's a girl, I don't know. Any suggestions?"

Carlotta remembered the fridge photo from her dream. "How about Lola?"

Hannah pursed her mouth. "Lola... I like it." She smiled, then angled her head. "You keep looking toward the door—are you expecting someone else?"

"Not really." She'd been hoping Tracey would stop by, but it appeared the woman didn't want to be in her life. And she couldn't blame her for not wanting to celebrate with her when Tracey's life was in shambles.

"Okay, it's your turn to have your palm read." She turned Carlotta in the direction of Madam Blue and gave her a little push. "Have fun."

Carlotta relented for her friend's sake. She didn't want to tell Hannah that she'd had her palm read once, inadvertently. A woman who owned a consignment shop had once told her that her life was in danger, and she'd been right. Carlotta didn't relish having her palm read again because she half-believed in the woo-woo stuff. And she didn't want a hit and miss premonition to mess with her mind.

She relaxed, though, when she sat down with Madam Blue. The woman's bejeweled costume and bright makeup were so over the top, so cliché, she couldn't be the real deal.

The woman smiled wide. "You are the bride, yes?"

And she had a fake accent to boot. "Yes, I'm the bride."

The woman pulled Carlotta's hand into her lap and studied it. "Hm... long love line... many paths."

Carlotta indulged the woman with a laugh. "Yes... my love life has been all over the place."

She turned Carlotta's hand this way and that, leaning in for a better look and running her forefinger along the creases. "Very unusual... very special."

She had to give her points for presentation.

"There were two men... no, three." She frowned. "No, two."

Carlotta's lips parted. "Two," she said to move things along.

The woman smiled. "Both good men."

"Yes."

"But one is… higher than the other."

"Higher?"

"Better, I think."

"One is better?" Carlotta laughed. "Yes." Even Jack agreed Coop was the better man.

"That's the one you're marrying, then, the best man."

She swallowed. "Let's hope so."

The woman smiled, then folded Carlotta's hand. "You have no need to worry… you will be happy, many children."

Carlotta smiled, relieved it was over and no calamities foretold. She thanked the woman, but walked away thinking she didn't need a palm reader to tell her she would be happy with Coop.

CHAPTER 30

"I'M SORRY this will be our last meeting," Dr. Denton said. "But I'm glad you feel therapy has gotten you to a better place."

"It has," Carlotta said. "I'm so grateful for your help these past few months while I worked through... so many things."

His eyes danced. "You have an interesting life, Carlotta."

"No offense, but I'm ready for it to be less interesting."

He shook his head. "I sincerely doubt that. Something tells me you will always choose the most exciting path. I'm here if you ever want to talk again."

She thanked him and shook his hand, but she doubted her life as a married woman would necessitate therapy.

When she walked through the lobby of the building, she glanced at a TV screen and stopped when she saw the news concerned Max Reeder.

"Heading into the last round of primaries, Governor Julio Pine is leading the pack, but Senator Max Reeder has been gaining momentum. Political pundits on both sides say Reeder has wide appeal among voters in all the important demographics. In Vegas, where oddsmakers have correctly predicted the last three nominees, Reeder is now a favorite. Flush with an injection of donations, the Reeders are set to embark on a nationwide campaign that will have the Senator stopping in every state in the Continental US."

Carlotta bit down on the inside of her cheek. If the Reeders had gotten wind that Colleen Mason's death might be revisited, being on the other side of the country would also help to distance them from the scandal. The clip showed footage of Max Reeder's most recent rally in North Carolina. He was dazzling as he waved to the crowd, and next to him, Delinda was radiant in one of the outfits Carlotta had chosen for her. The clip cut to the daunting size of the audience. It did seem that unless something happened to stop him, Max Reeder just might be the next President of the United States.

The camera panned the crowd in and around the stage where the Reeders stood waving. When she recognized a face among the staffers and security working around the Reeders, she gasped, then fumbled to snap a photo on her phone. Then she called Jack.

"Hi, Carlotta. I'm on my way into a meeting. What's up?"

"I just saw a clip of Max Reeder's last campaign rally, and guess who was there?"

He sighed. "Help me out here."

"Trevor Biondi, the guy from the valet stand at the Dallas airport."

"The one who talked to Patricia and knew where she was staying?"

"Right. When I tried to find him, he'd suddenly quit his job and supposedly moved to the West Coast. But from where he was standing on the stage, I'm thinking he's now on the Senator's payroll."

"Good pickup," he said. "I'll look into it. Now... focus on your wedding, Carlotta."

He ended the call and she frowned, then texted Jack the photo she'd taken, with a circle around Trevor Biondi's head. He sent back a wedding bell emoji.

She scoffed. When the heck had Jack started using emojis?

And it was hard to focus on the wedding when she had the nagging feeling that she possessed all the pieces to solve Patricia's murder—and maybe Colleen Mason's—but she hadn't yet figured out how they fit.

CHAPTER 31

THE HOTEL organizer clapped her hands to get everyone's attention. "Is everyone here?"

Coop looked to Carlotta. "Who's missing?"

"Just Jack," she said, scanning the rest of the wedding party. They all stood in the rear of the ballroom of the Georgian Terrace Hotel that had been partially staged to represent the way it would look tomorrow for the wedding. Carlotta's heart beat a tattoo on her chest... in less than twenty-four hours, she would be a married woman. "Maybe you should text him?"

Coop pulled out his phone and Carlotta flashed an apologetic smile to the organizer. "Everyone will be on time tomorrow."

The woman gave her a deadpan look. "Yes, that will be necessary for the wedding to take place."

"Jack is caught at work," Coop said. "He'll try to stop by later."

The organizer heaved a sigh, then waved everyone forward and began to bark out orders about where everyone would stand and the order of procession. Then she walked through the ceremony to let everyone practice. When Randolph walked her down the carpet toward where Coop was standing, Carlotta was captivated by the expression on her fiancé's face. Coop was so happy, and she was so happy to be the source of his happiness.

When the organizer was satisfied the ceremony wouldn't be a disaster, she dismissed them with a final warning not to be late, and directed them to the hotel restaurant for the rehearsal dinner.

Coop's parents were already seated in their reserved area. Carlotta loved them already—they were sweet and welcoming, and they patently adored their son. Both sets of parents seemed to be getting along famously, a good sign. Prissy sat between Coop and Carlotta, preening and primping to show off her new dress, and talking nonstop about the dress she'd be wearing in the ceremony. She watched Coop with her, how he patiently listened to every little-girl detail, and recalled the dream she'd had with the table full of mannerly children. He would be such a good father.

She took a moment to take in the people in the room—her parents, Wes and Meg, Prissy, Hannah and Chance, Coop and his parents. Her heart welled with love for all of them and gave silent thanks to have them around her at such a special time. Her gaze strayed to the door more than once, hoping Jack would show. At first she'd been perplexed and a little taken aback that Coop had asked him to be Best Man... but now she couldn't imagine getting married without Jack being in the room. Altogether, they rounded out to be a group of a dozen... twelve bodies who would ensure the wedding was all it was supposed to be.

"Don't worry, Jack will be here tomorrow," Coop murmured. "When it counts."

She nodded, then smiled and turned her attention back to the meal.

"Are you sure you don't want to stay here tonight?" Coop asked. "I can still book you a room."

She shook her head. "I still need to pack for London, and I'll sleep better in my own bed. Mom has my dress in her and Dad's hotel room. I'll drive over tomorrow in plenty of time to get ready."

He nodded and reached for her hand. "I can't wait for tomorrow."

She smiled and squeezed back. "Me too."

CHAPTER 32

"YOUR SISTER and Coop make such a good couple," Meg said, staring across to the head table.

"Uh-huh," Wes said, pushing down his concern. But if Jack had decided to sit out the rehearsal, maybe he'd bow out of the wedding, too... for everyone's sake.

"Thank you, Wes, for inviting me to the rehearsal dinner."

He turned his head and smiled. "Thank you for coming." His chest swelled with pride every time he introduced her as his girlfriend.

"Did I tell you how handsome you look in your suit?"

"Yeah," he said with a grin. "But you can tell me again."

She laughed. "You look very mature and sexy."

He leaned in. "Hm, does that mean I'll get lucky tonight?"

"Probably not," she said primly. "But there's always a chance."

He stared at her with awe—how was it possible that he loved her more every day?

"Are you okay?" she asked. "You seem... fidgety."

He wiped his mouth with his napkin. "I was going to wait until later, but... I got my SAT results."

She lit up. "How did you do?"

He reached into his inside jacket pocket and withdrew an envelope. "I haven't looked yet."

"Open it," she urged.

"Will you do it?"

She took the envelope and slipped her finger under the flap. As she pulled out the score sheet, he could hear his blood rushing in his ears. He needed a score of one thousand to get into any school that would have him, twelve hundred to get into an okay school, fourteen hundred to get into a good school.

At her silence, his stomach dropped. "Tell me... I didn't make one thousand, did I?"

She lifted a stricken look. "No." Then her face broke into a grin. "You scored a fifteen hundred!"

He blinked. "I did?"

When she turned the sheet around for him to see, he straightened. "I did!"

"This is so awesome, Wes. You have to tell your parents," she said, gesturing toward them two tables away.

"I will." He pushed to his feet. "But I have to call a friend first."

He strode out of the restaurant and stopped at the first quiet place in the hotel to make a phone call. When the call connected, Wes whooped. "Mouse? I did it!"

CHAPTER 33

CARLOTTA CLOSED the suitcase on her bed, then frowned when it wouldn't shut completely. How was she supposed to get two weeks' worth of clothes into two measly suitcases?

The first one wouldn't close either—she'd had to take clothes from that suitcase to put in this one.

Hot tears filled her eyes, but she brushed them away. Packing was not something to get upset over. Coop would have extra room in his bag. She took deep breaths to calm her nerves and forced herself to think happy thoughts. She was packing for a honeymoon abroad, for heaven's sake... she was the luckiest woman in the world.

Patricia would never have the chance to marry or to go on a honeymoon.

The sobering thought restored her equilibrium—she had so much to be grateful for.

She decided to lug the suitcases out to the Miata to clear her bed, and to have less to do tomorrow. When she walked past Wes's bedroom door, her heart swelled with pride. Even Coop had been impressed with Wes's test score. Her brother never ceased to amaze her.

When she opened the front door to the night air, exhaustion pulled at her. She'd been hoping to get to bed before now, but the rehearsal dinner had run long and she'd changed her mind three times about which outfits to take to London.

After wobbling her way down the steps, she hefted the suitcases down the short walkway to the garage and punched in the code to raise the door. The white Miata practically glowed in the low light. Since the suitcases wouldn't fit in the tiny trunk, she lifted them over the door and stacked them in the passenger seat.

Suddenly, it felt as if she couldn't take another step. And between thinking about the wedding and the new developments in the cases, she was mentally spent. She just needed to rest for a few minutes. She slid into the driver's seat, sighing when the soft leather upholstery cuddled her. Her heavy lids drifted down, sending her into fitful dreams.

When her eyes popped open, morning had dawned, and she remembered the last words of the wedding organizer—she couldn't be late!

She pushed herself up and out of the car, then hurried back to the townhouse.

"Carlotta!"

She grimaced, then turned her head to see her perennial neighbor standing at the fence. "Good morning, Mrs. Winningham."

"Maybe for you," the woman said, "but I want to talk to you about that husband of yours. He lets your grass get knee deep, and he gives my dog *bones*. I don't want Toofers to have bones!"

Carlotta squinted. She thought the woman loved Coop... and he'd never feed her dog without asking. "He's not my husband yet, Mrs. Winningham, but I'll talk to him."

She climbed the steps and pushed open the door. But when she smelled something burning, she ran to the kitchen to find a pan of scorched smoking bacon. She turned off the burner and waved her hands to clear the air. "Breakfast is burned," she yelled to Wes.

Jack walked into the kitchen, tying his tie. "What else is new?"

Carlotta gasped. "Jack, what are you doing here?"

"Running late, as usual. I'll try to mow the grass this weekend so Mrs. Winningham will stop harping on it."

He snagged a piece of charred bacon from the pan and took a bite. "Mmm-mmm," he said with a wincing smile. "I did not marry you for your cooking skills, that's for sure." Then he leaned in for a kiss. "But you have redeeming qualities. I think we should get busy tonight to see if we can coax this one to be born already." He patted her rounded stomach.

"Hm?" She stared down at her very pregnant belly. "How did this happen?"

He sighed. "Just like the other three. Birth control is only ninety-nine percent effective—we can't beat those odds."

At a noise from the living room, she looked up to see three boys in stair-step ages fly into the room yelling and shoving at each other. They were rag-a-tag dressed, hair sticking up at all angles.

"Good morning, kids," Jack said.

"Good morning, Dad, good morning, Mom," they chorused, fighting for the same chair.

"Did you make your beds?" Jack asked.

"Why?" they chorused.

"We'll just mess them up tonight again anyway," said the oldest boy.

"Good point," Jack said. "Homework all done?"

"No," they grumbled.

"Do it on the bus," Jack said, passing out Little Debbie cakes. "Who's the Mommy most likely to burn the house down?"

"Our mommy!" they cheered.

"Can we get McDonald's again tonight?" the youngest boy asked.

"You bet," Jack said. He pulled Carlotta to her feet and kissed her. "I'll try to be home on time, but I need to solve Colleen Mason's murder. Can you help me?"

"You want my help?" she asked.

"Of course." He pulled back. "What's wrong with your face, Carlotta?"

Her skin felt like a mask. She couldn't smile or frown.

"Carlotta?"

A phone rang.

"You'd better answer your phone," Jack said. "It's Coop."

The phone rang again… and again…

She opened her eyes to see she'd fallen asleep in the car again. From her pocket, her cell phone buzzed. She started to panic until she saw the clock—she still had time to get to the hotel to get dressed. She pulled out her phone to see Coop's name and connected the call. "Hello?"

"Are you okay? You haven't been answering your phone."

"I had it on vibrate... I just woke up."

"Good. I was hoping you'd get some rest. We have a big day ahead of us. Is everything okay?"

"I had another weird dream."

"Was it as good as the first one?"

She frowned. "Not really... but something in the dream triggered a memory." Her immovable face. "It's possible to die from a Botox injection, right?"

"Sure. Botox is botulinum toxin... if it's administered in high enough doses, it causes respiratory failure."

"Like Colleen Mason suffered?"

He made a thoughtful noise. "It's possible."

"Max Reeder's wife is a cosmetic surgeon. She'd have access to all the Botox she wanted. In fact, she offered to treat me."

He scoffed. "You don't need Botox."

She smiled. "That's sweet of you... but do you think it could be what killed Colleen Mason?"

"I'll have toxicology tests run while we're gone."

"Thank you," she said on an exhale. "I'm leaving for the hotel in a few minutes."

"I'll see you at the altar," he said, his voice vibrating with emotion.

"I'll see you at the altar," she said happily, then ended the call. After climbing out of the car, she stretched tall. The dream—ugh, what had Dr. Denton said about people trying out things they'd never do in real life? Even in dreams her relationship with Jack was utter chaos.

She walked back to the house to take a shower and apply basic makeup—she'd do her face up right when she got to the hotel. Throughout she kept marveling over the fact that today was her wedding day.

The happiest day of her life... so far.

She put on a casual, comfortable dress, checked her bag for essentials, then went to her office to get a safety pin from her desk. When she opened the drawer, her gaze landed on the photo of her and Patricia.

Her heart caught at the woman's elated expression. She wished she could go back and be a better friend to Patricia.

Then an idea slid into her head.

Maybe she could be a better friend *now*.

Carlotta rummaged to find Delinda Reeder's itinerary to see she was attending her last local event today, a luncheon at a Buckhead restaurant, before traveling across the country with her husband to drum up votes for the primaries.

She checked her watch. She had time before the wedding to try to do right by Patricia.

On the way out of the house she stopped in the kitchen to get the baggie with the used condom from the freezer.

Then she texted Jack. *Meet me at the Duck Wing restaurant in 30 minutes?*

A few seconds later, he responded. *Aren't you getting married today?*

Something I need to do first, I'll explain when you get there.

CHAPTER 34

"YOU'RE GOING to do *what*?" Jack's eyes bugged wide.

"Confronting Delinda Reeder with what I think happened to Patricia, and to Colleen Mason might give us what we need to prosecute."

"There is no 'we' here, Carlotta."

She gave him a pointed look.

He grunted. "You know what I mean. You're meddling again."

"Because I *can*. I can show her I have the used condom, and if it belongs to her husband, she'll want it back. You can't do that. I'll record the entire conversation on my phone, Jack. What could it hurt?"

He shook his head. "It could be dangerous."

"How? The woman is at a luncheon—she's not armed." She groaned. "Come on, Jack... we're already here. It'll take me fifteen minutes. If she reveals anything useful, I'll pass the recording to you, then I'll get married and hop a plane to London."

"And live happily ever after," he added lightly.

Her mouth tightened, then she closed her eyes briefly. "Let me do this for Patricia... please."

He heaved a long-suffering sigh. "Okay—against my better judgment. What's the plan?"

She gestured to the restaurant entrance. "I'll walk into the luncheon, and tell Delinda I have something to discuss with her in private. Easy, peasy."

"Right."

She suddenly noticed his disheveled clothing. "You don't look so good. We missed you at the rehearsal."

"Sorry... I've been working a case. I haven't slept."

She perked up. "Patricia's case? Colleen's?"

He closed his eyes briefly. "I got the footage from the hotel the night Patricia died. It shows Trevor Biondi arriving at the hotel with a black makeup case, and a few minutes later, he leaves with one."

She gasped. "So he did kill her! I'll bet Colleen hired him to swap the bags, and Patricia put up a fight."

"We don't know that," Jack said. "But we have enough information to bring him in for questioning... thanks to you."

She smiled. "Aw, Jack."

He checked his watch. "What time do you have to be at the hotel?"

"In thirty minutes... I have time to do this."

"Okay... let's get rolling so we can both... move on. But promise me if things start to go sideways, you'll walk out."

"I promise. You'll wait for me here?"

He hesitated, then nodded and leaned against his car. "I'll be here."

She felt a blip of sympathy for him—he looked as if he'd rather be taking a nap. She gave him a last look, then turned and walked into the restaurant, wearing her best smile.

"Hello," she said to hostess. "I'm here for Delinda Reeder's luncheon."

The woman checked her watch. "The luncheon is almost over."

"I know, I was delayed. I won't be eating," she said, then patted her purse. "I'm just dropping off a check."

She pulled out a list. "Your name?"

"Carlotta Wren. My name isn't on the list, but Delinda knows me. And her assistant Emma."

"Follow me."

Carlotta walked with the woman to a private dining room where the luncheon seemed to be wrapping up. When Delinda spotted her, she waved, so the hostess let her in.

"Carlotta, what a nice surprise," Delinda said. "How are you?"

Carlotta's pulse tripped higher. She couldn't reconcile the woman in front of her with a woman who'd take someone else's life. "I'm fine. Actually, Delinda, I wondered if we could have a moment in private?"

Delinda smiled, then gestured to a corner of the room. "Of course, we can step over here."

"I was thinking the ladies' room—I have something of your husband's you might be interested in seeing."

The woman's face hardened, but the fact that she didn't ask for more details told Carlotta she'd had similar conversations before. "I'll have Emma clear the ladies' room so we can talk," she said in a cool tone. She signaled her assistant, then murmured something for her ears only. Emma gave Carlotta a chilly stare, then walked into the women's restroom. A few seconds later, she came out and nodded to Delinda.

Emma parked herself next to the door to serve as a lookout. Carlotta followed Delinda into the ladies' room, where the woman's demeanor instantly changed. "Show me your phone." She offered up a flat smile. "No recordings."

Of course the woman would be on guard. When Carlotta held up her phone, Delinda took it from her and turned it off before handing it back. Change of plans—she wouldn't have a recording, but she might still get some useful information.

"What's this item of my husband's you think I might be interested in?"

"A used condom," Carlotta said, pulling the baggie from her purse and holding it up. "That belonged to Colleen Mason. Does it look familiar? Maybe from a photo she sent to you asking for blackmail money?"

Delinda's eyes turned frigid. "How do you know that woman?"

"It doesn't matter. This is the DNA she was going to go public with, before she was murdered."

"The woman committed suicide."

"No, she died of respiratory failure... I think from a Botox injection you gave her."

A muscle worked in the woman's temple. "That's totally preposterous. I would never do such a vile thing."

"The sad thing is, you didn't have to," Carlotta said. "Because Colleen lost the DNA she was using for leverage. It's why she suddenly stopped talking to the press. Plus at that point she had bigger problems. She hired Trevor Biondi to get the DNA back from someone who didn't know they had it, and that innocent person wound up dead." Carlotta's jaw hardened. "That innocent person was a friend of mine."

Delinda narrowed her eyes. "So you manipulated your way into our lives."

"No," Carlotta said. "A happy coincidence... maybe it was the universe trying to set things right."

"This is crazy talk," Delinda said, heading toward the door. But she lunged for the baggie containing the condom.

Carlotta yanked it back. "I've talked to the police, and to the Medical Examiner. Colleen Mason's body has been exhumed to be re-autopsied."

Delinda lifted her chin. "I didn't kill that woman."

The door opened and Emma walked in, then reached into her jacket and withdrew a handgun. Fear rose in Carlotta's chest, then Emma swung the gun toward Delinda.

Delinda gasped and backed up to the wall. "Emma, what are you doing?"

Emma's eyes were empty. "She made me do it," she said to Carlotta.

"That's a lie," Delinda yelled.

"She went to meet with Colleen Mason at her home under the pretense of paying her hush money. Instead she slipped painkiller into her drink and when Colleen started to feel the effects, Delinda demanded the condom. Colleen said she'd lost it, that a woman had taken the bag it was in by mistake and the idiot she'd hired to retrieve it had accidentally killed the woman. She begged for her life, but Delinda loaded up a syringe of Botox, and made me inject her with it." Emma's throat convulsed. "We stayed until she stopped breathing."

"Shut up!" Delinda screamed.

"Then you tracked down Trevor Biondi," Carlotta said, "and put him on your payroll. You thought you'd tied up all the loose ends."

"Except for me," Emma said. Her hand shook. "I'm sick of covering up for your family."

"Emma," Carlotta said gently, "don't do this." But the woman had to know she was headed for prison.

"They never learn," Emma said. "All of the Reeders just keep doing bad things to mess with other people's lives."

Tears slid down the woman's cheeks... Carlotta wondered if the son had also used her.

"Put the gun down," Delinda said. "Emma, we can work through this."

"No, we can't," Emma said, then turned the gun on herself.

"No," Carlotta screamed and dove for the woman's legs. A shot fired and Carlotta heard the ricochet as she landed on the hard tile. The gun slid across the floor. Under her, Emma moaned, so at least she wasn't dead.

Carlotta scrambled after the gun, but Delinda got there first. She picked it up and pointed the barrel at Carlotta. Her smile was regretful. "You should've let her kill herself. Now I have to finish off both of you, and blame it on Emma, let her take the fall one last time."

She leveled the gun and Carlotta realized with a swell of grief she wasn't going to make it to the wedding after all.

The door burst open. "Freeze," Jack yelled at Delinda. "Drop the gun." When she didn't immediately lower it, he grunted. "I *will* shoot you, lady. Drop it *now*."

Delinda dropped the gun, then sank to her knees. Jack moved in and kicked the weapon under a stall, then holstered his gun and handcuffed Delinda.

"They both killed Colleen Mason," Carlotta supplied.

Emma lay in the floor sobbing. Jack used a cable tie to secure her wrists, then turned to Carlotta. "Are you okay?"

She nodded, then went to him. He held her close and she could feel him shaking.

"Jack—"

"Don't say a word. Just let me hear you breathe. As soon as backup arrives, we'll leave. You're getting married today."

CHAPTER 35

"JESUS CHRIST, you cut it close, didn't you?" Hannah said, practically dragging Carlotta into the dressing room.

"We thought you'd run away," Prissy said.

"Or were kidnapped," Hannah added. "Or you were dead. That would've put a serious damper on the reception."

"I... had to take care of some unfinished business," Carlotta murmured. "I'll fill you in later."

"The important thing," Valerie said, "is that you're here now."

Carlotta gathered them all to her for a group hug. "For a long while I've been preoccupied with... other things, but now I can focus on what I know will be the happiest day of my life."

"Yeah, yeah," Hannah said, wiping her hand over her moist eyes. "Let's get the show on the road."

"Right," Valerie said, pointing to the dazzling gown with the riotous train. "It's time to get you into that dress."

"This will be a feat of engineering," Hannah mumbled.

Carlotta laughed, still rattled from the run-in with Delinda Reeder and Emma Wallace, but limp with relief that she'd made it to her wedding.

Thanks to Jack.

"Time to get married," she said, wiping her own happy tears.

She surrendered to the helping hands and allowed herself to be pushed and pulled and prodded. It took all of them to get her into the wedding gown and veil and to arrange it around her, but when she stood in the mirror, she knew it was a triumph.

"Wow," Prissy breathed. "It's the most beautiful wedding dress ever made."

"It's beyond spectacular," Valerie said, dabbing at her eyes.

"It needs its own zip code," Hannah declared.

A knock sounded at the door. Valerie went to answer it, then looked back to Carlotta. "It's your father, can he come in?"

Carlotta nodded, then smiled wide when Randolph appeared, so handsome in his tuxedo. Valerie shooed out Prissy and Hannah, giving her a private moment with her dad. Her heart welled over for the man who had loved her and instilled in her the strength to become a strong, independent woman.

"You are a vision," he said, blinking back tears. He kissed her cheek. "Are you ready for this?"

"Yes," she said. "I'm ready for the next chapter in my life." It was true. So much of the last ten years had been about getting Wes raised and finding her parents. She was ready to start living her own life.

Randolph sighed. "I feel as if I only just got my daughter back, and now I'm supposed to give her away."

"To a man who will love me as much as you've loved mom."

He nodded. "That's the only way I can bear to let you go, sweetheart."

A rap sounded and the wedding organizer peeked in. "I don't think we can delay much longer."

Randolph extended his arm to Carlotta. "Shall we?"

She nodded and walked with him to the door, where Valerie waited with her bouquet of three perfect white calla lilies. Her mother pressed a final kiss to Carlotta's cheek, then followed Prissy and Hannah to line up with the rest of the wedding party.

From where she and Randolph stood, Carlotta could hear the uplifting chords of the string trio that had entertained the guests longer than planned. When the music shifted to the prelude song, her heart began to race. At this very moment, Coop was standing at the altar, waiting to make her his wife. Prissy would be making her way up the aisle, dropping pink rose petals as she basked in her moment.

Then Jack would escort Hannah to her spot as Maid of Honor—she only hoped the two of them could make it that far without trading barbs—and he would take his place next to Coop.

Then Coop would walk back to escort his mother down the aisle to her seat, and Wes would walk their mother to her seat.

The music dipped, then swelled to a wistful high note... and then the wedding march began to play.

"That's our cue," Randolph said, squeezing her hand.

Carlotta moved her feet. She tried to remember to smile, but she was having trouble breathing. It all felt so surreal. When they walked to the doorway of the ballroom, she gasped. Since the rehearsal last night it had been transformed into a magical setting of white and pink and silver. She distantly registered they were choices she had made, but the moment seemed dreamlike, as if it were happening to someone else.

The guests stood to honor her, then a murmur traveled among them when they caught sight of her gown. Carlotta felt like a princess floating down the aisle toward her prince. Coop was tall and handsome in his tux, beaming at her. Jack and Wes were more reserved, staring at the floor and the ceiling respectively. They both looked resplendent in their tuxes. The minister smiled and nodded along with the music.

Seeing Hannah's grin helped her to relax enough to glance at guests on both sides of the aisle. She smiled at June and Rainie, and seeing Jolie was a nice surprise. Mrs. Winningham waved as if they were old friends. Lindy was there, and other former coworkers, including Quentin. She recognized friends of Coop's and friends of her parents, and Wes's girlfriend, plus Chance. But the face that surprised her most was Tracey's—and she was wearing the red scarf. Carlotta nodded to her, fighting back tears.

As they neared the end of the aisle, she focused on her smiling groom and how in just a few moments, they would pledge to love and honor each other until death parted them.

Her step faltered.

Thankfully, with the enormous train, only her father could tell.

"You okay?" he whispered.

She nodded, then found her footing. Everyone felt like this on their wedding day, she reasoned—as if they were having an out of body experience.

Right?

For some reason, her gaze went to Jack for reassurance, the person who had calmed her nerves before, and who'd thought her wedding was important enough to break every traffic law to get her there on time.

But Jack didn't appear to be feeling well. He was sweating profusely and shifting side to side, no doubt suffering from the night of lost sleep and the stress of foiling an attempt on her life. Affection for the man who'd always been there for her flooded her chest, as well as grief for his personal losses that had frozen his heart. If only—

The processional music trailed off, and Carlotta suddenly realized she and Randolph had reached the end of the aisle. Her father kissed her, his eyes shining with pride, then he went to stand next to Valerie. Carlotta handed her bouquet to Hannah, then took her place next to Coop...

Where she would be until the day one of them died.

Carlotta tried to take a deep breath, but the dress was constricting her lungs.

Coop gave her a bolstering smile, and she exhaled. This was what she wanted.

Next to Coop, Jack was using his handkerchief to mop at the perspiration on his forehead. Carlotta hoped he didn't pass out.

"Dearly beloved," the minister said in a deep, rumbling voice that reverberated through the room, "we are gathered today in this beautiful venue to witness and bless the union of Carlotta Wren and—"

"Stop," Jack said.

Carlotta pivoted her head to him and stared, as did everyone else, although she distantly registered that Wes had his eyes squeezed shut.

Coop looked stricken. "Jack."

"Coop," Jack said in a strained voice, "I'm sorry, I should've spoken up sooner—"

His words were cut short when Coop's fist connected with his jaw. The crowd gasped and the minister dropped his book. Jack stumbled back and let another punch fall before he slugged Coop and they fell to the ground. Stupefied, Carlotta shrank back as men in the audience rushed forward.

Wes blocked their way. "Stay back. This has been a long time coming. Let them duke it out."

"I agree," Hannah said, standing with Wes. "Let them fight to the death."

Carlotta didn't realize she'd retreated down the aisle until she was near the door she and Randolph had entered. The two men were still rolling around on the ground, trading blows. Some guests were standing on chairs for a better view. Carlotta felt numb. Her perfect day had disintegrated.

She lifted her voluminous train, then made a run for the exit.

CHAPTER 36

OUT OF the corner of his eye, Wes saw Carlotta make a run for it. He ground his jaw and swallowed a mouthful of curses. The happiest day of her life, spoiled by two men who were supposed to care about her. She must be devastated.

He blamed himself. He'd seen this coming, had been watching Jack wind himself tighter and tighter as the wedding had drawn closer—he'd known the man was ready to blow. He should've warned Coop... or Carlotta. Instead he'd hoped Jack would do what most dick-swinging alpha guys did when it came to expressing emotion—opt to let it eat them alive.

The tuxedoed pair were still flailing away at each other like two angry bucks who didn't realize the doe had fled.

Wes looked at Hannah. "That's enough, they're just embarrassing themselves now."

Hannah harrumphed. "Okay, you get Coop, I'll get Jack."

Not for a minute did Wes doubt that a pregnant Hannah could pull Jack away from a fight. They circled the men, then went in— Wes with a bearhug, Hannah with a chokehold. They dragged the men apart just as hotel security came running in.

"We're good," Hannah said, waving them off. "Just a little wedding brawl between friends." Then she signaled the traumatized wedding organizer. "You might want to set up an open bar and ask the band to strike up something cheery. This could take a while to sort out."

Jack and Coop both looked worse for wear—they were bruised and bleeding from scratches and busted mouths, their clothes torn and stained. The two men glared at each other.

Coop wiped his hand under his bloody nose. "I should've known you were going to pull something like this, Jack. You can't stand for Carlotta to be happy, can you?"

When he said Carlotta's name, it was as if the men suddenly remembered she was supposed to be there.

Coop craned his neck. "Where is she?"

"Where's Carlotta?" Jack parroted.

"She left," Wes said, jerking his thumb toward the exit.

Hannah looked back and forth between the men. "Did you think she was going to stay and marry the idiot who was left standing?"

Jack looked miserable. "I didn't exactly think it through."

"What should I do?" Coop asked Hannah. His face creased with anguish as the gravity of their actions descended. "She must hate me."

"She doesn't hate you," Jack said, sounding tired. "She was going to marry you." He looked pained. "I didn't mean for this to happen. You need to go after her, Coop."

CHAPTER 37

CARLOTTA LET the tears fall freely as she drove north on Peachtree toward the townhouse. She didn't care that she created a spectacle with mascara running down her checks and her wedding dress overflowing the Miata. Fortunately, the convertible was small enough for the valet to squeeze around the limousine she and Coop were supposed to take to the airport to fly away to their honeymoon.

She cried harder as realization began to set in that now none of those things were going to take place.

She blamed herself. Deep down, hadn't she known something like this would happen? The two men had been trading verbal slings over her since she'd first met them. Even Coop asking Jack to be his best man now seemed like some kind of one-upmanship. Had he been daring Jack to interfere? And since the day Jack had bared his soul to her, hadn't she sensed things would come to a head?

She could've stopped it. She should've asked Jack to bow out of the wedding party, or insisted that she and Coop get married without all the fuss.

Or convinced Coop that he was her first and only choice so he didn't feel as if he had to set up a showdown to be sure of her heart.

Instead they had subjected their family and friends to a public confrontation that would lead to what? Just because Jack didn't want her to marry Coop didn't mean he wanted to marry her himself, or even commit to her. More likely, he wanted to preserve the fantasy that she would be available to him.

Behind her, horns sounded. She glanced in the rearview mirror to see a black limousine threading through traffic. She bit into her lip. Coop was coming after her.

Of course he was. He would apologize and persuade her to return to the wedding where everyone was waiting. They could pick up where the ceremony had left off or start over and proclaim their love and commitment to each other, just as they'd planned, then dance at the reception and run through a shower of birdseed as friends and families sent them off to start their lives together.

The limousine moved closer, was four cars behind her, and the driver was still honking the horn.

She turned and waved to Coop to let him know she saw him. Around them other drivers were connecting the dots between the crying bride in the convertible and the streamer-decorated limousine following her. Cars pulled over and maneuvered to let the limousine pull up behind her. She put her car in park and smiled, telling herself how lucky she was to have someone like Coop to love her.

She had to make things right.

Because underneath the hurt and the humiliation and the tears, another emotion had emerged when she'd burst through that exit door.

Utter and abject *relief.*

By the time the valet had brought the car around, she'd retrieved her purse from the trunk of the limo, removed her engagement ring and dropped it inside.

She couldn't marry Coop, not when her soul yearned for another man. Coop was a lovely, wonderful person, but when she'd met him, her heart had already been snagged by Jack Terry. She just hadn't realized it at the time.

From the moment she'd met Jack and they'd sparred over Wes's arrest, her life had changed. He'd electrified her then, and he electrified her still. What was the line Hannah had quoted? *The heart wants what it wants.* When she was in trouble or lonely or had good news to share, her mind always went first to Jack. He'd behaved badly, had dragged her heart through fire, but she wasn't perfect either, and not always easy to love. But no matter what, he had been ever-present in her life.

The rear door to the limousine opened and she steeled herself to break Coop's heart. He deserved more than a woman who would always be wondering what if about another man.

When he climbed out, she squinted in the mirror, then her lips parted. It wasn't Coop.

Jack.

Her heart expanded in her chest, but she swiftly tamped down her reaction. For all she knew, he could be coming to take her back to Coop.

Jack strode up to the driver's side of her car, then leaned both hands on the door. His face was bruised and bloodied, and his tux was in disarray.

"I made a mess of things."

An understatement of gigantic proportions, but she simply nodded.

His gold-colored eyes were dark with desperation. "Dammit, Carlotta... I've been in love with you since the first time I laid eyes on you, but I didn't want to be. I pushed you away and I convinced myself you were better off with Coop." He hesitated, then gripped the door so hard his arms shook. "But I can't bear to see you make a life with someone else... if there's a chance that you want to make a life with me."

Her heart brimmed with unspeakable happiness, but after all the emotional acrobatics this man had put her through, she wasn't ready to put him out of his misery just yet.

He closed his eyes briefly. "Please say something. Is it too late for us?"

"No," she said finally, covering his hand with hers. "Our life begins now, Jack."

His expression lifted, then a grin slowly overtook his face.

Next to them, a driver leaned out the window. "For Pete's sake, kiss her already."

"Kiss her," someone else shouted.

"Kiss her! Kiss her!"

Jack leaned down to capture her mouth for a passionate reunion, a reconnecting of their minds and bodies. He was hers... she was his.

He lifted his head and his eyes bored into hers. "Marry me. Today. Now."

She laughed, incredulous. "Now?"

"Why not? We're dressed for it."

Carlotta took in the horns and cheers around them, then lifted her hands. "Okay, let's do it."

Jack grinned, then signaled the limo driver to leave and opened her door. Then he frowned. "I don't think there's room in your car for me and your dress."

"I love my dress," she pouted.

"I love the top part of it," Jack said, wagging his eyebrows. He offered his hand to help her step out against the pull of the mountain of fabric. "Does the train come off?"

"It's not supposed to."

He reached down and yanked at the seam where the train was sewn to the dress at the knees. A wrenching rip sounded, then he kept pulling. The curlicue train fell away a few inches at time as he circled her until only the body-hugging white mini-sheath remained.

"That's better," he said, devouring her legs.

She mourned the mound of gorgeous white tulle piled on the sidewalk for a couple of heartbeats, then lifted her face to Jack. "Let's go get married."

CHAPTER 38

JUDGE HONDO leveled his gaze on Jack. "Jack Terry, do you take this woman to be your lawfully wedded wife?"

Carlotta's heart tripped with anticipation, but to her delight, Jack didn't hesitate. "I do."

The black-robed man smiled. "I believe hell just froze over."

Brooklyn, their last-minute witness, laughed. "Good one, Judge."

Jack gave them both a withering look. "Can we continue please?"

The judge turned to Carlotta. "Carlotta Wren, do you take this man to be your lawfully wedded husband?"

She savored the two words she'd only dreamed of exchanging with the man in front of her. "I do."

"Do you have rings?" the judge asked.

"Yes," Jack said.

"Jack, place the ring on your bride's finger and repeat after me."

Brooklyn held out the gold bands they'd hastily purchased at a pawn shop near the courthouse. The novelty endeared the ring to Carlotta even more. It was fitting that she and Jack have an unconventional ceremony.

Jack slid the ring onto her finger and repeated after the judge. "Before these witnesses I vow to love you and care for you for as long as we both shall live."

He spoke the words carefully and with conviction. When the man loved, she realized with wonder, he loved deep.

"Carlotta, place the ring on your groom's finger and repeat after me."

Carlotta slid the band onto Jack's big hand, awash with the gravity of the sacred ceremony. "Before these witnesses I vow to love you and care for you as long as we both shall live."

The judge closed his book and beamed. "I pronounce you husband and wife. You may kiss to seal your union."

Jack pulled her into his arms for a deep, hard kiss. Brook and the judge clapped for them. Jack shook the judge's hand and accepted a hug from Brooklyn.

"I knew you were smarter than you looked," Brook said, pounding him on the back.

Carlotta felt as light as air, giddy with happiness. "Where to now?" she asked Jack. She couldn't wait to be alone with her husband.

Jack's eyes hooded with desire. "There's a by-the-hour hotel on the next block. Want to book an hour?"

Carlotta smiled. "How about two?"

He grinned and pulled her toward the entrance, waving goodbye to their witnesses. They practically ran to the Miata and were at the seedy little hotel in record time.

Before the door to the room could close behind them, they were undressing each other.

"I promise I'll take you somewhere nice for a honeymoon," Jack said, unzipping her abbreviated white dress.

"I'm counting on it," she said, pushing off his tuxedo jacket.

He shimmied the dress over her head and pushed down the tiny white lace panties to her ankles for her to step out of. When she started to slip off her satin high heels, he stopped her. "Leave them on."

He shrugged out of his dress shirt, and tossed it aside, then shucked off the tuxedo pants and underwear, all at once.

Carlotta sucked in a breath at the sight of the big nude body she hadn't seen for a long while. He lifted her and she wrapped her legs around his waist. He buried his face in her cleavage, then walked to the bed and lay them both down.

"I've missed you," he whispered on her neck.

"I'm here now," she murmured. "And always."

Jack kissed his way over her breasts and down her body, awakening every nerve ending. When he reached the valley between her legs, she cried out and dug her nails into his shoulders. She gasped his name and arched into his mouth, riding the wave of bliss. Before she could recover, Jack had climbed her body.

"I can't wait any longer to have you," he said in a hoarse voice. He pulled her knees to his waist and thrust into her. Their moans mingled as they adjusted to each other. When Jack began to stroke inside her slowly, the restraint on his face filled her with satisfaction. She loved knowing she affected him the way he affected her—their physical chemistry had always been untamed.

He kissed her, swiping his tongue into her mouth, giving her air and taking it back. His kiss grew more hungry and insistent as his body pistoned in and out of hers. Everything he did to her drove her to higher heights. His uniquely intimate knowledge of her body coupled with the fact that this man was her forever lover brought another climax to the surface quickly. She clutched at his back and moaned into his mouth while her feminine muscles pulled him deeper inside her. With one massive thrust that welded their bodies together, he groaned his release and pumped into her, sounding like a man who'd been put out of pain. His heartbeat drummed against hers.

After they recovered, Jack lifted his head. "I thought married sex was supposed to be bad."

"Not ours," she said, giving him a playful jab.

He rolled to his back and panted for air. "You will be the death of me."

She laughed. "Not for a while, I hope."

He sighed, then picked up her left hand and put it next to his. Their wedding bands glowed in the low light of the lone window. "We really did it."

"We really did," she agreed.

"I feel... happy," he said in an odd voice, as if he'd never expected or deserved to be.

She folded their hands together. "I'm happy, too, Jack... more than any woman should be."

"Let's keep doing this," he said.

Carlotta gave a little laugh. "Having sex?"

"Well, yeah. And making each other happy… without trying to change each other."

Her heart unfurled. "Agreed."

They kissed to seal the deal. From his pile of clothes on the floor, the ring of a phone sounded.

"Damn," he said. "I forgot—I'm on call."

"Answer it. I know how demanding your job is."

He pushed to his feet, then retrieved the phone. "Hello?" As he listened, he began to reach for his clothes. "Okay… can you send a unit to pick me up? I'll text the address."

She sighed, then smiled. This was what she'd signed up for… and she was proud to be married to a man who made a difference in other people's lives.

He ended the call and grunted. "Sorry… there's been a murder in Alpharetta."

At the mention of the upscale area in the suburbs, she made a rueful noise. "That's terrible. And unusual."

"Yeah, that's why I caught the call."

"What happened?"

"A wealthy woman was strangled in her home—" He stopped, then pointed his finger. "Don't do that. You can't be nosy about my cases."

"But I'm your *wife*, Jack."

"Exactly." Then he softened. "I'll tell you about it when I come home, okay?"

Home. She brightened. "Okay."

He checked his watch. "There's still time on the room if you want to relax. Meet you back at the townhouse?"

She nodded, already looking forward to his return. She climbed off the bed and walked over to get a goodbye kiss. "But we're going to have to sort out our housing situation, Jack. We can't live with Wes, and I'm not sure I can live on a boat. I need a bigger closet."

He squinted. "How do you know I live on a boat?"

She bit into her lip, then looped her arms around his neck. "Quick, kiss me."

He clasped her mouth in a sweet, savory kiss, then lifted his head. "We'll talk about this later, Mrs. Terry."

Her heart hitched, loving the sound of that.

When the door closed, she hugged herself and gave a little squeal. When she'd opened her eyes this morning, she'd thought today would be the happiest day of her life, but she couldn't have imagined just how happy.

She took a quick shower and wrapped a thin towel around her. Then she sighed and pulled her phone from her purse. Over a hundred calls and text messages from Wes and her parents, but mostly from Hannah. It was time for damage control.

She connected a call to her friend, who answered before it even rang.

"Where the fuck are you?"

Carlotta gave a little laugh. "I'm in a fleabag hotel near the courthouse. Jack and I just got married by a Justice of the Peace."

In the silence that followed, she knew her friend was working up to an explosion.

"*What?* How did *that* happen?"

"He came after me. He proposed. I said yes."

"So that's where he disappeared to."

"Yeah. So what exactly happened after I left?"

Hannah sighed. "The two of them rolled around like schoolboys until Wes and I broke them up. Jack apologized to Coop and told him to go after you. But Coop said it was foolish of him to get between you two in the first place. After that he announced to your guests the wedding was off, and asked the organizer to start the reception. Everyone stayed, except Jack. I assumed he was going out to get drunk."

Carlotta grimaced. "I'm sure Coop hates me for leaving."

"You know that's not Coop. He's hurt, but he'll recover. I saw Rainie consoling him at the reception."

"And my parents?"

"Wes told your folks not to worry, that you could handle anything. Everyone seemed to be making the best of a regrettable situation. Prissy was on the dance floor teaching the Electric Slide. Chance and I left early because I needed more to eat than finger food."

"Thanks for helping to smooth things over, Hannah."

"No problem." Her friend sighed. "I guess I shouldn't be surprised you and Detective Dickhead wound up together."

"You have to stop calling him that."

"No I do not. I'm surprised, though, that he let you come up for air on your wedding night."

"Jack was called out on a high profile murder in Alpharetta. We're supposed to resume, um, wedding-night activities later."

"That must be the same call I received for a body pickup. I guess the morgue is short-handed since so many people are still at the reception. I have to call back and decline since I can't do it on my own."

Carlotta pushed her tongue into her cheek. She kept a change of clothes in the trunk of the Miata. "I could help."

Hannah scoffed. "Won't that be a little sticky now that you're the wife of a police detective?"

She pictured the expression on Jack's face if she showed up at the crime scene. "Yes."

"Cool. Pick you up in ten minutes?"

Carlotta smiled into the phone. "I'll be ready."

-The End-

A NOTE FROM THE AUTHOR

THANK YOU so very much for reading 12 BODIES AND A WEDDING! Ending the Body Movers series has been a bittersweet experience—I've had these characters in my mind for more than fifteen years so they feel like friends and family to me. As you might imagine, I wrestled for a long time with how the series should end and which man would ultimately capture Carlotta's heart. To be honest, I swung back and forth many times before deciding how to give Carlotta her happy romantic ending. Even as I began writing this book, I had reservations, but as the story progressed, I felt better and better about what seemed to be the inevitable conclusion. I'm sure there will be readers who wish the story had gone another way, but I hope you know I didn't make the decision lightly.

And that brings me to you, dear reader. Without your patience and support, the Body Movers series would have ended years ago in an abrupt, unsatisfying way. But because you continued to read the books and spread the word about the series, Body Movers has enjoyed a loyal following that continues to grow as new readers discover the books. I don't have words to thank you for allowing me to more fully develop the characters and storylines I started with. I hope you are pleased with the way the series has evolved over the years, and with how things wrapped up. Thank you for coming along for the ride—I couldn't have done this without you.

Are you signed up to receive notices of my future book releases? If not, please visit www.stephaniebond.com and enter your email address. Thanks again for your time and interest, and for telling your friends about my books. As long as you keep reading, I'll keep writing!

With gratitude,
Stephanie Bond

OTHER WORKS BY STEPHANIE BOND

Humorous romantic mysteries:
COMEBACK GIRL—*Home is where the hurt is.*
TEMP GIRL—*Change is good... but not great.*
COMA GIRL—*You can learn a lot when people think you aren't listening.*
TWO GUYS DETECTIVE AGENCY—*Even Victoria can't keep a secret from us...*
OUR HUSBAND—*Hell hath no fury like three women scorned!*
KILL THE COMPETITION—*There's only one sure way to the top...*
I THINK I LOVE YOU—*Sisters share everything in their closets...including the skeletons.*
GOT YOUR NUMBER—*You can run, but your past will eventually catch up with you.*
WHOLE LOTTA TROUBLE—*They didn't plan on getting caught...*
IN DEEP VOODOO—*A woman stabs a voodoo doll of her ex, and then he's found murdered!*
VOODOO OR DIE—*Another voodoo doll, another untimely demise...*
BUMP IN THE NIGHT—*a short mystery*

Body Movers **series:**
PARTY CRASHERS (full-length prequel)
BODY MOVERS
2 BODIES FOR THE PRICE OF 1
3 MEN AND A BODY
4 BODIES AND A FUNERAL
5 BODIES TO DIE FOR
6 KILLER BODIES
6 ½ BODY PARTS (novella)
7 BRIDES FOR SEVEN BODIES
8 BODIES IS ENOUGH
9 BODIES ROLLING
10 BODIES LYING
11 BODIES MOVING ON
12 BODIES AND A WEDDING

Romances:
LOTTERY GIRL—*Maybe money can buy happiness?*
FACTORY GIRL—*Long hours, low pay, big dreams...*
COVER ME—*A city girl goes country to man-sit a hunky veterinarian who's the victim of a "cover curse"!*
DIAMOND MINE—*A woman helps the one who got away choose a ring—for another woman!*
SEEKING SINGLE MALE (for the holidays)—*A roommate mixup leads to mistletoe mayhem!*
MANHUNTING IN MISSISSIPPI—*She's got a plan to find herself a man!*
TAKING CARE OF BUSINESS—*An FBI agent goes undercover at a Vegas wedding chapel as the Elvis impersonator!*
IT TAKES A REBEL—*A former hotshot athlete is determined to win over the heiress to a department store empire who clashes with the new spokesman—him!*
WIFE IS A 4-LETTER WORD—*A honeymoon for one... plus one.*
ALMOST A FAMILY—*Fate gave them a second chance at love...*
LICENSE TO THRILL—*She's between a rock and a hard body...*
STOP THE WEDDING!—*If anyone objects to this wedding, speak now...*
THREE WISHES—*Be careful what you wish for!*

The Southern Roads series:
BABY, I'M YOURS (novella)
BABY, DRIVE SOUTH
BABY, COME HOME
BABY, DON'T GO
BABY, I'M BACK (novella)
BABY, HOLD ON (novella)
BABY, IT'S YOU (novella)

Nonfiction:
GET A LIFE! 8 STEPS TO CREATE YOUR OWN LIFE LIST—*a short how-to for mapping out your personal life list!*
YOUR PERSONAL FICTION-WRITING COACH: *365 Days of Motivation & Tips to Write a Great Book!*

ABOUT THE AUTHOR

STEPHANIE BOND was seven years deep into a corporate career in computer programming and pursuing an MBA at night when an instructor remarked she had a flair for writing and suggested she submit material to academic journals. But Stephanie was more interested in writing fiction—more specifically, romance and mystery novels. After writing in her spare time for two years, she sold her first manuscript; after selling ten additional projects to two publishers, she left her corporate job to write fiction full-time. To-date, Stephanie has more than one hundred published novels to her name, including the popular COMA GIRL serial, and STOP THE WEDDING!, a romantic comedy adapted into a movie for the Hallmark Channel. Stephanie lives in midtown Atlanta, where she is probably working on a story at this very moment. For more information on Stephanie's books, visit www.stephaniebond.com.

COPYRIGHT INFORMATION

CPSIA information can be obtained
at www.ICGtesting.com
Printed in the USA
LVHW111143050522
PP17324900004B/4